Superior

Zoe Amos

Superior: Adventure Romance
   by Zoe Amos

Paperback:
   ISBN 10: 0-9844394-5-5
   ISBN 13: 978-0-9844394-5-4

E-book:
   ISBN 10: 0-9844394-4-7
   ISBN 13: 978-0-9844394-4-7

Published by:
   Good Day Media
   P.O. Box 1007
   San Marcos, CA 92079

www.GoodDayMedia.com
info@GoodDayMedia.com

Cover design by Janet F. Williams
Interior design by William Metcalfe
Editorial services by Lois Winsen, editorontap.com

First edition: November 2013

Acknowledgements:

I wish to express my thanks to my editor, Lois Winsen, whose keen eye and astute suggestions make my writing flow. I cannot express highly enough the gratitude I feel for the effort you put in to make my writing a work of art. Your support keeps me chugging along. I also wish to thank all of my pre-publication readers, in particular, Julia Carson, Rhonda Shapiro, and Tamar Berg. Your comments allowed me to see the trees in the forest and helped me craft a better story. A special thank-you goes to Sid March for remembering my work and allowing me to reach readers on www.lesbian.com.

Chapter One

No one decides where or when they are born, and no one knows when it will be their time to leave this earth. Seven years after Civil War II, a baby was conceived in Superior Protectorate and nine months later Miss Kristian Browne was born. Miss Kristian's father had told her the story of her birth. She was breach, and though the skilled doctors at Marquette General Hospital were able to turn her around for a natural delivery, her mother, Mrs. Zarah Browne, lost a lot of blood. Fortunately, Miss Kristian was healthy. She was chipped, scanned, and sent home. Mrs. Browne remained weak. Finding enough donors for her rare blood type was a challenge, and during the forty-day quarantine she died. Mr. Browne was allowed to perform the service at sea, as per the rules set in place at that time. Lake Superior doesn't give up its dead.

Mr. Browne was assigned a nanny to care for his daughter. When Miss Kristian came of school age, the Protectorate decided she would spend her years with other girls in similar situations attending The Academy in Superior City, formerly known as Munising. It was for the benefit of all. Mr. Browne would not have thought to argue. He missed her and during visits he took comfort knowing she thrived in the company of the other girls at the boarding school under the close watch of her women keepers.

At commencement, Mr. Browne stood proudly at the dais when Miss Kristian's name was called. He marveled at her beauty and the resemblance to his late wife. Miss Kristian's blonde hair hung low down her back in a carefully braided plait. She was almost six feet tall and carried herself well. Wearing the traditional modest clothing of older girls did little to hide her muscular physique earned from labor in the cornfields. She was a fine example of budding womanhood and Mr. Browne beamed as the director handed him her diploma. He would keep it with her few possessions until it was time to pass them on to her husband once she married. At the conclusion of the ceremony, he put his arm around her shoulder and pulled her close.

"Let's get punch," he said.

It was a clear day and a tent had been set up outside on the grass. They walked beneath it, served themselves food and drink, and spread cheer with other families. It was a time for hugs and good-byes. Many of the women would be heading home for the summer, a short respite before starting trade school or university.

"Where's Miss Rhona?" Miss Kristian asked, referring to her friend.

Mr. Browne laughed. "We can't leave without her, now can we?"

Miss Rhona's parents had died in a squatter's raid after the war, and as his daughter's long-time friend, Mr. Browne had tried to pick up the slack by providing a summer home for the girl.

Miss Kristian blushed. There was never enough time when she was with Miss Rhona. She scanned the area until she saw her friend from the back. Miss Rhona preferred a double braid, and though her hair was thin, the ends touched her rounded behind in a teasing manner. At that moment, Miss Rhona turned slightly and Miss Kristian caught sight of the port wine stain splashed across her neck that disappeared into her high collar. Others had made rude comments, especially when they were children, but Miss Kristian thought the deep red coloring made her stand out in an interesting way. Now she wished she were touching Miss Rhona's neck, and more.

Chapter Two

M r. Browne worked at the animal feed mill in Marquette and he took the girls with him into town on the community shuttle. Summer jobs were scarce and to accommodate as many people as possible, the office work was shared on a rotating schedule. Miss Kristian worked Monday and Thursday, Miss Rhona worked Tuesday and Friday, and another woman worked Wednesday and Saturday.

It was a summer of unknown freedom. Miss Kristian spent her hours when she was alone practicing her home skills. She would need them one day to make a happy home for her husband. She enjoyed cooking and sewing. She requested material and was given enough to make drapes for her father's sitting area and kitchen. As thriftiness was considered next to godliness, she sewed the scraps together and made two patchwork pillows. Miss Rhona helped her do the piecework and they surprised Mr. Browne with the unexpected gift. The delight was apparent on his face, and he picked one up and hugged it tenderly as a child would a beloved stuffed toy.

Each Sunday they dressed for church and were greeted at the entrance by the minister, his wife, and their six children. Services were augmented by community participation. Miss Kristian marveled at the precision it took to make her visits seamless. All congregants had their assigned tasks and much was done out of sight. She and Miss Rhona had been asked to help in the kitchen. After services, they headed downstairs and were given cakes to slice or cookies to put on trays.

"I hear you girls are going to a farm camp," the minister's wife said. "You'll be cooking for the hands, no doubt. What a treat for them."

"I've signed on as labor," Miss Kristian said.

"And I'll be in the lab," said Miss Rhona, "I hope."

"And they're allowing it? You're not children any more."

"Yes, ma'am," said Miss Rhona. "It's a new program in Escanaba. The Protectorate sees benefit. So be it."

"I suppose it doesn't hurt to do these things. It's only for two years. You girls will find husbands there. Then when you settle on their share, you could help out until you're chasing after your little ones, eh?"

Miss Kristian looked at Miss Rhona and bit her lip. Then she looked back at the minister's wife. "Yes, ma'am."

When their kitchen tasks were finished, the girls stood in line for their allotments. Mr. Browne would have already received his algae fuel for the kitchen stove. Food for three meant more variety than he enjoyed the rest of the year, and the girls enjoyed cooking for him. As they unloaded the goods at his house, it set Miss Kristian to wondering.

"Father," she asked, "after mother died, why didn't you take another wife?"

"I loved your mother too much," he said.

"Didn't you ever think about it? Don't you get lonely?"

"No, I never think about anyone else, except you, of course. Knowing you're safe and cared for is all I need." He smiled at her as he put boxes away in an upper cupboard. "Mr. Findlay asked about you," he added.

"Well, I'll see him next week. I'm sure he'll find a reason to come into the office. He always does."

"He's a nice young man."

"I'm two years away from my marrying year. Is that all anyone thinks about?"

He shrugged. "You brought it up."

She wanted to admit to her father the feelings she felt for Miss Rhona, but that would only cause trouble for everyone. Young men were immature. They said stupid things and she couldn't imagine falling in love with any of them. Their hairy bodies were unappealing and when they returned from the fields they smelled acrid, like crushed skunk cabbage. On the other end of the spectrum was Miss Rhona who possessed everything she would ever want from another person in life. Her love was deep and it pained her to know that if anyone found out about the times they stole away to kiss, they would be separated—or worse.

There were rumors about men and women who secretly tried to couple with others of the same gender. Sometimes those people were never heard from again, or so the stories went. For her own safety and Miss Rhona's, Miss Kristian kept her thoughts to herself. She did nothing that would cause a raised eyebrow. When they brushed against one another during casual contact, it was hard to keep her hands to herself. They shared a room like sisters and never whispered at night. One never knew who might be listening.

Summer weather bore down hot and sticky the day the girls packed their few belongings in readiness for their trip to the Escanaba farm camp. There, they would be issued new clothing. It was a comfort to know everything would be provided, as it always was. Ever since its formation, the Protectorate lived up to its promises for food, clothing, shelter, and work assignments. Being physically strong added to Miss Kristian's impressive academic record and made her a good candidate for the new labor program. Mr. Browne thought it would match well with his daughter's mechanical interests. Miss Rhona was small for her age and not very strong. Because she had no parents to guide her, Mr. Browne spoke up for her. He thought the transition would be easier for both girls to move into the new environment together. Miss Rhona excelled in science and displayed a strong ability to focus on projects. Determination was a positive character trait and helped ensure her inclusion in the program.

On the day of departure, the girls boarded the community shuttle with Mr. Browne. At the church, Miss Kristian could see buses lined up, their destinations in block letters posted in the front windows. Piles of luggage were mounded in small hills and Mr. Browne made sure their bags were in the correct loading zone. The girls saw others they knew and shouted good luck messages. Mr. Brown checked their papers one last time and hugged them good-bye. Miss Kristian felt his sense of pride and loss through his tight smile and watering eyes. She didn't know how long it would be before he could visit.

At the farm camp, the girls were directed to their dorm and assigned rooms. Miss Kristian took the bottom bunk, leaving the top for nimble Miss Rhona, who practically flew up the wooden steps. The other bunk bed was empty. While on the bus, Miss Kristian noted two women travelling with them; the rest were teenaged boys, some of whom she recognized from town. Other girls would be coming in from across the Protectorate and would help fill out their numbers. It was exciting for her to think about the close relationships she would form with her eventual bunk mates. They would form a new sisterhood.

After a short while, the new arrivals were herded inside a lodge with a large open room for an assembly. Refreshments were served and the two were seated with four other girls. A handful of women stood nearby. Otherwise, the room filled with older teenaged boys. From the looks of the tanned arms and lined faces of the men who stood off to the other side of the room,

Miss Kristian thought they must have seen many seasons at the farm.

"Am I on?" A man's voice came over the address system and Miss Kristian saw the speaker standing to the right of the men's section. "Greetings! I'm Mr. Harlingen, the farm camp supervisor. To familiarize you with your new home, we'll be showing a holovid. You'll be introduced to your assigned keeper who will give you a tour of the grounds. Some of you chose to be here and others were chosen, and we're happy to have everyone. While you're here, you'll learn, you'll contribute, and you'll make the Protectorate a better place to live. So be it."

A holovid, a three-dimensional image projected against a white backdrop, appeared near the front of the room. Miss Kristian watched the overview of her environs showing the lodge and surrounding dorms, the planted acreage, warehouses, silos, and such. The area was scenic, and showcased the beauty of the four seasons. A semi-transparent holographic image of Mr. Harlingen's body appeared superimposed over the aerial shots. It created an odd effect, making it seem as if he floated in midair as he narrated. Miss Kristian wondered why they chose to mix technologies when regular 3D Pixelmation would have sufficed.

The lodge was not air conditioned like the office at the feed mill, and the body heat from those in attendance warmed the room. Sweat formed beneath her arms and across the top of her neck. When the holovid ended, it was a relief to go outside and feel a breeze. A squat woman gathered the girls and led them a short way along a path. She was heavy-set with thick ankles showing beneath her calico dress, but she had a spring to her shuffling gait that made Miss Kristian believe she was heartier than she first appeared. She stopped and turned to face the six eager faces huddled around her.

"Well, girls," she said, "this is your new home. I'm your keeper, Mrs. Porter, and also the camp nurse. My husband, Mr. Porter, is a keeper for young men. We'll be looking out for you, guiding you, and making sure you have what you need. This is an experimental program, so I'm counting on you to make it a success. Now, come along and I'll take you through the warehouse."

Miss Kristian followed as they passed through the warehouse littered with old farm equipment. The next building contained the mechanics' bays. Miss Kristian nudged Miss Rhona with her elbow, her smile indicating her excitement about her work assignment to keep the equipment running. Unlike most of the other girls at boarding school, Miss Kristian had shown an early interest and aptitude as an engine mechanic. Her size and strength gave her an edge over her classmates. She stood eye-to-eye with her instructor, a middle-aged man from Detroit whose idea of the good life included the purr of an old-fashioned V-6 engine. Miss Rhona's specific work assignment in the algae lab had not come through. As the tour continued, the girls eagerly eyed the woodworking studio, laundry, lodge kitchen, and the rows of huge generators that powered the farm.

Mrs. Porter took them back to their dorm and explained shower limits. The six girls became acquainted. There was Miss Betsy from Iron Mountain, Miss Trudia from Sault Saint Marie, Miss Julie from Ishpeming, and Miss Analise from Superior City.

"When will the other two girls be joining us?" asked Miss Rhona.

"There was a change in plans," Mrs. Porter said. "Two girls were sent to Superior City. I don't know if they'll be coming later."

The girls glanced at one another. Superior City, the capitol since the war, had much to offer. An assignment could mean a quick rise in standing and the prospect for a good marriage. It could also be a sentence for wrong-doing, and judging by the edge in Mrs. Porter's voice, Miss Kristian had a feeling it might be the latter.

The group walked to a supply room where Mrs. Porter issued extra clothing. Miss Kristian returned to her dorm where she spread the new items out on the bed for review. The bell tone for dinner sounded, but she took a moment to feel the heavy denim overalls between her fingers, so unlike the summer dresses and winter leggings she had worn her young life. They would take some getting used to, as would the heavy work boots. She couldn't wait to try them on, but dutifully headed to the dining hall in the lodge where dinner would be served.

The girls sat together at their assigned table with Mrs. Porter at the head. During dinner, Miss Kristian was aware of the other boys trying not to be obvious as they stole glances their way. Miss Trudia spilled soup because she was busy looking out of the corner of her eye instead of focusing on the bowl in front of her. In time, Miss Kristian knew she would get used to her new surroundings and meals with boys would seem commonplace. During summer breaks, she rarely interacted with the few boys who lived near her father. There was no intermixing at the girls' boarding school she attended, no dances or other occasions with exposure to boys her age. There were field trips to the ice cutter museum and quartz mines where her class was segregated from other co-ed groups on tour. She had limited contact with the older men running the school, though she knew what it was like to be in the company of her father. It was a good feeling and gave her hope. Inevitably, she would be coupled and her man would provide a deep love that would endear him to her. In the meantime, being in the same room with boys was good practice.

At the sound of the morning tone, Miss Kristian was already awake. She got up and put on her long-sleeved shirt, overalls, and work boots in preparation for her first full day. Except for her shirt, the clothes felt heavy. After breakfast, she walked to the mechanics' bays to check in. A group of young men stopped talking as she entered. They stared at her and a few looked stunned.

"Where are your manners, boys?" a man said as he strolled in behind her. "Have you forgotten how to address a lady? Good morning, Miss. I'm Mr. Taybert." He extended his hand and she shook it. "You and these youngsters will be keeping our fleet going, that is, if they can remember how to behave. They act as if they didn't know you were coming. Boys, this is Miss Kristian. My report says she tuned up the bus fleet at her boarding school. I don't see special recognition for many of you."

A young man jumped to the front of the crowd. "Nice to meet you, Miss Kristian," he said. "I'm Mr. Stewart."

Miss Kristian shook each boy's hand as they introduced themselves in turn. Some of them flushed red and others were startled by her firm grip. She towered over half of them. For now, they were to work side-by-side as equals. Older men were at work and noise in the bay took over as hydraulic tools buzzed in the background. Mr. Taybert took his new crew of twelve on a detailed tour and then posted work assignments. They would work in teams, beginning with general maintenance of the corn pickers.

She was relieved when handed another uniform, a blue mechanic's shirt and pants. It fit well with the belt snug around her waist. Her shoes were black leather, thick-soled, rounded at the toes and steel enforced. They clomped as she walked toward her group.

Mr. Taybert explained how the corn stalks and shucks produced dust, and when combined with dirt, the corn pickers were subject to clogs and excess friction that wore on moving parts, making them less efficient. He directed them to the steam cleaner and greasing tools. He taught them how to inspect for bent and broken parts, though repair would be left to others.

Late summer was the middle of corn picking season. Seeds had been planted every two weeks from late winter through August, and the current crop was fresh and good. Warm days would continue, even with the sun heading south. The last crops were planted with Quick Grow, best suited for the dwindling sun hours of autumn. Bred for sugar content, it was suitable for ethanol production, not for consumption. The tough kernels had a thick exterior that protected it from an early Canadian cold air mass. It could thrive in light snow and was a boon to the Protectorate whose promise of self-sufficiency was key to survival.

Miss Kristian got busy and soon lost track of time. She was startled when the late afternoon tone sounded. Back at the dorm, she took her turn in the shower and donned her dress for dinner.

Miss Rhona came in a few moments later and sat next to her.

"I'm working the algae tanks," she said.

"That's good! You got what you wanted."

"Not exactly. I'm not in the lab. There are several large tanks filled with algae, and an open framework surrounds each one. In the winter it's enclosed, so it's a year-round operation."

"Oh. Well, maybe by then you'll be promoted to the lab. I'm cleaning corn pickers. There are pickers that only pick the ears, picker-huskers, picker-shellers, and more, and they all need maintenance. I don't suppose they're going to put me on engines the first day."

Miss Rhona nodded. "Yes, I need to be grateful. We made it!"

Miss Kristian smiled back. They were together and that was the most important thing. They could have ended up on opposite ends of the Protectorate doing kitchen work or helping out with someone else's children. They squeezed their hands beneath the table and then recited their meal prayer.

Zoe Amos

Chapter Three

M iss Kristian settled into a routine at her work station. She worked alongside three boys tasked with the same job—cleaning and greasing corn pickers. Mr. Stewart, who introduced himself to her first, kept a watchful eye. She wondered if he was angling to find fault, but there were no errors to correct. He spoke to her often, whereas the other boys paid her no special attention. In the evening during quiet time, she discussed it with Miss Rhona.

"He's like a hawk in the field, waiting for me to slip up so he can swoop down and chew me up. You can't say they didn't warn us. You would think we would gain credibility with our knowledge, but only some men give us that benefit. They don't like us doing their work, even for a little while. I get the feeling they want us to fail, even though the Protectorate sees benefit."

"I've got a fellow like that, too," Miss Rhona replied. "Mr. Kowalski. He doesn't like me. I'll be minding my own business, running the strainer through the algae or moving it into the next holding tank and he'll be watching me with a scowl on his face."

"Do you think we should report it?"

"What for? It's like you said, most men don't believe what girls have to say outside the home. It would only create a problem where none exists. Eventually, we'll be given our next assignment. If I get into the lab, I probably won't have to work with him, and you'll probably get separated on your next assignment, too."

Miss Kristian looked thoughtful. "You're probably right. If it's important, I'll find out what's on Mr. Stewart's mind, and then I'll know if it makes sense to tell Mr. Taybert. He's supportive of my being there and wants our program to be a success."

Her opportunity came sooner than she imagined when walking through the fields with Mr. Stewart on the way to a corn picker stranded in a field. At first, Mr. Stewart walked ahead, but Miss Kristian's long legs kept pace. He slowed and walked by her side. He became chatty about the work in the shop and what they might find wrong with the corn picker. It seemed he wanted to say something else and she wondered how she might respond to an accusation, especially with Mr. Taybert out of earshot. She noticed he was getting closer and his arm brushed her shoulder. Miss Kristian moved aside to give her companion room, but he startled her by grasping her arms and kissing her on the mouth. She pulled aside in shock.

"Mr. Stewart!"

"It's okay out here," he said. "No one's watching."

He pulled her to him. She pushed him away.

"That's not the point!"

"Don't you know how I feel about you? Since the day we met, I knew you could be my wife." He tried to kiss her again, but she shoved him into the corn. He fell, and his back rolled against a dirt berm enabling him to stand up again in one swift motion. He lunged at her for another try. "Don't fight me. Kiss me! Kiss me and tell me you think about me as much as I think about you."

She positioned her forearm against his neck and forced him back. "So that's what you're about—the way you look at me all the time."

"You do notice! I knew it! Miss Kristian, I go after what I want. I'll be running a large tract one day. You'll like being my wife." He came toward her in slow steps. She balled her right fist and ground it into her left palm. She had never been in a situation where she had to defend herself. He stopped.

"I'm two years away from marrying age," she said, "and I didn't come here to get sent away because you couldn't wait. I'm sure Mr. Taybert could separate us in the meantime." She snorted in anger and planted her feet solidly in the dirt.

"No! No, Miss Kristian! I would never! I didn't mean...I don't want you to think I would do anything like that. Just a kiss. It's all I think about and there are always folks around. No one's here in the field. A tiny kiss?" He raised his brows high and his face softened, conveying he hoped she would see things his way.

"I can't help the way you feel," she said, "but I don't think about you."

"Is there another boy?"

"No." She thought of Miss Rhona. "I'm not ready."

"I'm sorry," he said. "I was hoping you might feel differently. And maybe you will someday. In the meantime, I'll keep my sights on you. I'll protect you."

They resumed their walk. Miss Kristian slowly let down her guard and thought about his words. She didn't know much about boys, but he seemed sincere. In a cornfield of men, it would not be a bad idea to have a protector.

In a few moments they came upon the disabled corn picker. Mr. Taybert was there talking to the driver. The problem was in the tractor and not the picker, which was attached to the rear. The four of them disengaged the components and waited for another vehicle to haul away the tractor. When the next tractor arrived, they hooked up the picker to it. The tractor roared and moved along the unfinished row. They stood back and watched as it stripped the corn from the stalks, unseen metal fingers doing work she had performed by hand during summers at the boarding school.

At quiet time, Miss Kristian lay face up on her bunk. She raised her leg and nudged the underside of the top bunk with her foot.

"What?" Miss Rhona asked as she peered down over the side of her bunk.

"Mr. Stewart tried to kiss me today. I fought him off."

"You mustn't say that. Someone could hear and you could get into trouble."

Miss Kristian got out of bed and stood so her head was next to Miss Rhona's. "No one suspects anything between us." She kissed Miss Rhona lightly on the lips before returning to her bunk.

During free moments after the evening meal, the girls found opportunities to sneak away into the hidden cover of the cornfields where they could express their affection. Tall stalks provided an effective shield against prying eyes. There, they shared small kisses and cuddled, or simply held hands and talked. Miss Kristian's heart pounded when kissing Miss Rhona, and not only because of the risk of getting caught, though that would be serious. Discovery of inappropriate behavior would mean expulsion from the farm camp with one or both of them sent to Superior City for retraining. Or, they might be separated and never see one another again.

All too soon, the harvesters gathered up the last of the Quick Grow stalks. Now the fields were open and one could see great distances across the flat land. Cold weather had bared its icy teeth on more than one occasion, and ethanol fueled heaters warmed their dorms and work spaces. In many respects, it was a typical winter with several snow storms dropping four to six inches of wet snow. A New Year's ice storm stopped work temporarily, but the predictable January thaw brought rain that melted the icicles hanging from the eaves.

Around the algae tanks, the PlastiCorn panel enclosures created a humid, greenhouse effect. The inside air, heavy with moisture and combined with the stale odor of algae, made it seem more like a sultry late summer day. Miss Rhona observed as boys around her left one by one for other work assignments. Her worries over Mr. Kowalski disappeared when he took his promotion in the filtration house. Boredom set in to her daily schedule as she strained the algae. Surely the Protectorate would see the benefit of placing her in the lab.

For her part, Miss Kristian had assisted in winterizing the farm equipment, which allowed her to peek inside the giant engines, drain the oil, and steam clean in preparation for late winter sowing.

During this period of slowed activity, Mr. Harlingen called more assemblies and invited family members for daytime visits. On one such occasion, Mrs. Porter's husband gave a presentation on life before the days of the Protectorate. Mr. Browne came and visited with his daughter. Miss Kristian had missed her father and was thrilled to see him. During the presentation, he sat between his daughter and Miss Rhona. The lecture included photographs taken decades before the war when average winter snowfall was six feet and temperatures stayed below freezing for weeks at a time. The audience gasped at the sight of a cabin with snow drifts covering the roof. This was followed by an old color photograph of a snow-suited individual with an ice-encrusted moustache pointing at a thermometer registering twelve below zero.

"Didn't know then it would change so much," Mr. Porter said, "or so fast. We heated our cabins with wood stoves, and used propane tanks and gas forced air, not understanding the value of our natural resources. We stripped the copper and iron ore without thinking about what we were doing to our environment. Fortunately, we left a lot of the quartz. Our ignorance became our salvation." The audience murmured in agreement.

"Climate change laid the groundwork for our future. When the Great Lakes receded, people got scared. Shipping, fishing, and fresh water supplies were threatened. The so-called "Water Wars" started. When the Atlantic coast and Gulf States flooded beyond what anyone could imagine, refugees overran the Upper Peninsula where they camped in the mountains and burned our trees. They slaughtered our wildlife to survive and polluted the water for the rest of us downstream. The refugees brought lawlessness and we were headed toward ruin. Who can forget the raid on Gladstone? Maybe some of you have visited the memorial there.

"Like the first Civil War in the United States, the north, in this case, Canada, wanted peace with their neighbor and trading partner to the south. During Civil War II our peaceful land turned into a terrorist state until Canada stepped in. No one argues that point. By securing our borders, they secured a long stretch of their own. After all, they had their hands full with illegals pouring in from the States and elsewhere. We're fortunate Superior Protectorate became a sovereign nation.

"We've seen what can happen when we ignore the natural laws of the land. Without the Protectorate, we'd be like the rest of those sorry lots in the United States who live in tent cities with poor prospects for the future. It took almost three more years after the war to flush out all the squatters hiding in our hills and abandoned mines. We broke up their hierarchies and the raids on our towns finally stopped. Our long-standing conservative values and new political structure allow us to take care of our own. We produce food and make energy the right way. And we have peace.

"I'm sure you know by now Mrs. Porter and I are native Menominee. After Civil War II, we had the choice to stay or go live with family in Wisconsin. We knew we would have to do things differently here, do what the Protectorate told us to do. Mrs. Porter and I were born here. We love this land and we wanted to see it prosper. If the Protectorate had been here long ago, we wouldn't be trying so hard to catch up and repair the damage caused by the others. By the grace of God you've been given a gift to live here and work here." He thrust his fist into the air for emphasis. "When the Protectorate tells you to do something, it's for the benefit of all!"

"So be it!" members in the audience called.

"Here's a photograph of me and Mrs. Porter on our snowmobiles. We were kids, like you. We burned gasoline for fun. Now we know better."

After the presentation, Mr. Browne spent some time with Mr. Porter while the girls chatted with the parents of their dorm mates. The late afternoon sun dipped low and Mr. Browne bade his good-byes with hugs for the girls.

Rain continued through February and filled the reservoir. Muck filled the soles of Miss Kristian's shoes as she tromped to the mechanics' shed to start her next assignment—checking engine computers for warning codes. It wasn't a difficult task, and she was glad to be inside while the weather was still unseasonable.

"You're lucky," Miss Rhona said as they headed toward the lodge for dinner. "They're promoting you. How can I serve when all I do is move algae from one tank to another?"

"It's an important job. We need algae. It keeps us healthy and we need the fuel."

"They promote the boys. I'll be moving algae for two years."

"I'm sure it'll be soon," Miss Kristian said.

"And I'll be of marrying age before you. No promotion and then, I don't want to think about it."

"Meet me?" Miss Kristian whispered her code phrase to spend private time with her love. She smiled warmly, hoping Miss Rhona would forget the unpleasantness of her current situation and focus on something they both enjoyed.

Miss Rhona smiled back. That evening, Miss Rhona would join her on the lower bunk where they could cuddle and forget the hard work of the day. The extra bunk in their dorm remained unoccupied, and as long as they were quiet, they would not have to worry about someone hearing the sweet sounds of their kisses or the compliments they murmured to one another in the dark.

In the morning, Miss Kristian woke first. Her nightgown had wrapped around her leg and she arranged it so as not to wake her friend. She looked at the angelic face of her love. There was no tension in Miss Rhona's face as there had been the day before. She felt sorry things couldn't be different. It was entirely possible Miss Rhona would never be promoted. It was more important for the boys to move ahead. One day they would both be married and it would mean a good life to marry a man with a promising career. The women would have to wait until the children were grown to take on another job, and by then, likely thirty years from now, whatever they learned at the farm camp would be dated and of limited use.

She didn't like to think about having a husband, not for herself or for Miss Rhona. It was not important for her to have children, though she assumed she would have the obligatory two. She would want them to be sweet and smart like Miss Rhona. Their friendship began in the early days at boarding school. Miss Rhona never teased about her height like some of the others had, and Miss Kristian admired her friend's joy in living that spilled over into the wonders of the natural world. It came as no surprise that her friend's curiosity led to the bio lab where her scientific interest melded with a deep appreciation of the outdoors.

It was easy to remember what Miss Rhona looked like as a child. Many of her features still carried a youthful quality and Miss Kristian wondered if Miss Rhona's children would look like her or her chosen husband. She wished she and Miss Rhona could be a married couple, but of course that was impossible. She reflected upon the talks given at boarding school about same-sex couples. No one knew for sure what befell them when they were discovered. Some were sent to Superior City and could rejoin society after they proved themselves worthy. What happened to the others? Did they escape to Canada or what was left of the United States? Perhaps they were never heard from again because they were silenced. Questions by those who dared to ask them, were cast aside by keepers with admonishments to behave. She had a vague recollection, a rumor about one such fallen woman sent off to marry a quartz miner near the western border. These thoughts caused Miss Kristian to tighten her embrace.

Miss Rhona stirred and awakened. She opened her eyes and smiled when she saw Miss Kristian. She nuzzled her face into Miss Kristian's neck and exhaled softly. Their lips met and Miss Rhona closed her eyes. An angel in dreamland, Miss Kristian thought. My angel for now; no matter what is to come.

They roused themselves out of bed. Miss Rhona hopped onto the top bunk and smoothed her unused covers. The two gathered their towels and went to the showers. Miss Trudia exited and they nodded to one another. As she passed by, Miss Kristian noted a bruise on the side of Miss Trudia's neck.

Chapter Four

March wildflowers bloomed in a profusion of color. They popped up everywhere—in the fields separating the common areas, in between the crops, alongside the roads, in the forests, and on the way back from church. Miss Rhona picked a bunch and placed them in a cup in their room.

"How pretty! And sweet as you," Miss Kristian said.

Miss Rhona smiled and tilted her head downward. She peered at Miss Kristian coyly. The others would be back from church soon, but that seemed of little consequence. Miss Kristian shut the door to their room and they embraced. She felt a wave of emotion and kissed her friend with unknown passion, not just on her lips as they had done many times, but on her face and neck. Her hands found their way onto Miss Rhona's bodice and she walked her backward toward the wall. She leaned into her using the weight of her body, her long fingers smoothing the curves of Miss Rhona's womanly figure. Appreciative noises spurred Miss Kristian to rub against her in a way girls were not taught to do, yet felt natural. Miss Rhona responded in kind. Miss Kristian threaded her fingers through her friend's hair, grasping the strands in her fist as a surge of excitement tingled between her legs. She stopped when she heard voices. The others had entered the common area outside their rooms. Her breath was heavy near Miss Rhona's forehead and she noticed Miss Rhona's breath had also quickened. She backed away and handed Miss Rhona a hairbrush, and though they continued their afternoon as though nothing unusual had happened between them, there was no denying something had changed.

The next day as she walked toward the mechanics' shed, Miss Kristian took better note of her surroundings. She knew the immediate area well and began to wonder what lay beyond the shed. Were there trails in the forest worth discovering? Vegetation was growing higher as each successive day warmed. Deer jumped out of the shadows with spotted fawns trailing behind. Dense forest greenery made good cover. It set her to thinking about things she knew could cause trouble, but she could not stop herself.

In the mechanics' shed, Mr. Taybert directed her toward a stuck window on one of the older tractors. She climbed into the driver's seat about eight feet up from the ground. The enclosed glass cab had air conditioning and the window was stuck open. She needed to fix it before the driver could go out for the day. It was jammed sideways and off-track. Carefully, she worked the window back and forth until it slipped nicely down. She cleaned and greased the track, and then lifted the window up and down a few times to be sure it wouldn't cause another jam.

"Good job, Miss Kristian," Mr. Stewart said as looked up into the cab. "Now I can get my lesson."

"You?" she replied.

"Why not me?" He extended his hand to help her down. She held onto the grips and pushed off, landing near him as he stepped aside. "You're a real do-it-yourself type. I like that. You could drive this, if they'd let you."

"Women don't drive. You're the one who needs to know. You'll be growing corn, right?"

He smiled. I already know how to drive a tractor. My father has a large tract near the Soo," he said, referring to Sault Saint Marie. "I'd like to show it to you someday. I could teach you how to drive."

"Really? Hmm," she nodded.

Mr. Taybert joined them. "All fixed?"

"Yes, Mr. Taybert."

"Hop in the passenger seat, Mr. Stewart. We're going for a ride. Miss Kristian, ask the men working in bay number four if you can clean up."

"Yes, Mr. Taybert."

She walked to bay four and offered her janitorial services to the men.

"No, Miss. We won't be done for a few hours yet. Why not take a walk on a beautiful day and come back after lunch?"

The roar of a tractor starting caught her attention and she saw Mr. Taybert drive off with Mr. Stewart. She followed behind into the bright sunlight. It was unusual for her to have free time during a work day, and before the men could change their minds she headed down a dirt road. Wanting to get out of sight, she walked through a high meadow and into a copse of aspens that called to her with the undersides of their flickering, spade-like leaves that caught the sun. The forest was dense with aspen, oak, maple, pine, and cedar, and she hesitated to explore until she spotted a path, an animal trail leading into the interior. She followed it, and when it split in two she took the right fork. After a time, the forest opened up into an idyllic meadow. To mark her place, she bent a small branch down and meandered into the open field. Midway through she spotted a flattened area where a deer had spent the night. Here, she rested on her back.

The sky was a beautiful aqua blue and puffy clouds scudded along. Redwing blackbirds flitted from tree to tree along the edge of the meadow. She picked a piece of grass and chewed the end, sucking on the sweet green that released between her teeth. She imagined she was a deer running free, loping along forest corridors known from memory, with no schedules to keep and no unwanted husbands.

A deer could wander at will within the sealed boundaries of the Protectorate. There was the heavily guarded northeastern border at the Soo, the restricted Mackinaw Bridge that crossed to the south into Michigan, and the western border wall that kept sinners from the United States from entering and destroying the Protectorate. The Great Lakes were also guarded with the help of the Fleet.

The lakes were cold, even in summer, though Lake Michigan was tolerable. In the years before she was born, Lake Superior would freeze over during the winter. Ice cutters, heavy-duty ships with thick bows and herculean motors could break through ice over thirty feet thick to open shipping lanes, and sometimes even they got stuck. Now, with the warming, shipping lanes on all five lakes were open year-round and the cutters were only used in the bays and rivers. Many years ago, a deer could cross the ice in winter. And though deer could not leave the Protectorate, they weren't chipped. She felt the bean-sized implant in her forearm lined up next to the long tendons running parallel along her wrist. No one kept track of deer.

She laced her fingers behind her head and replayed her last moments with Miss Rhona. Her love had been longstanding, and now there was something new and exciting to consider. She couldn't wait to see her again. She wanted to hold her and touch her everywhere. Tonight, she imagined them together, skin against skin. They would have to remain absolutely quiet. It would be a risk, one worth taking for love. Her heart pounded against her chest at the thought of touching Miss Rhona beneath her nightgown. She imagined Miss Rhona must be thinking the same thing and how it would feel to have her friend's hands exploring her body in the dark of night. Before she could get too carried away with passionate ideas, she decided to rise and head back before the lunch tone sounded. On the way out, she marked the trail with lengthwise branches so she could find her way back again.

To her dismay, Miss Rhona was not at lunch and the other women did not know her whereabouts. Minutes dragged by as she chatted amiably.

"Have you heard?" Miss Julie said, "A new group is coming in."

"I saw a bus this morning," said Miss Analise. "I'm so excited!"

"That's right," said Mrs. Porter. "We're expecting a new girl. We'll finally fill out our dorm, or almost. You and Miss Rhona," said she to Miss Kristian, "will finally get a bunk mate."

"Oh!" Miss Kristian covered her shock with a forced smile. "What a surprise! Wonderful!"

"It's about time," said Miss Trudia. "I'm used to a large sisterhood."

"Me, too," said Miss Betsy. "I miss my sisterhood. Now that they're mining quartz, Iron Mountain has grown. You wouldn't believe all the people walking around town. My parents say they hardly recognize it."

Just then Miss Rhona came in, all smiles and bouncing. "Sorry, I'm late. I'm starving. Guess what? I have the best news! I got promoted!" She took her seat next to Miss Kristian and the others passed the food bowls her way.

"That's great," said Miss Trudia. "We have some news, too. A new group came in, and you and Miss Kristian are going to have company."

Miss Kristian could see the news hadn't quite sunk in. "We're getting a bunk mate. Another girl will be sharing our room." She emphasized the clarification.

Miss Rhona had taken a bite of a corn fritter and for a second, stopped chewing. She swallowed the chunk. It pressed against her throat like a rock. Her eyes watered and she took a few sips of lemonade to force it down. She looked at the faces surrounding the table, landing on Miss Kristian.

"How about that?" Miss Kristian said, as if she couldn't be more delighted. "We're going to meet a new sister. Now, tell us about your promotion."

Miss Rhona cleared her throat. "I knew we had some new boys come in. One of them took my job at the algae tank. I was showing him the straining tools. That's why I was late."

"What's your new job?" asked Miss Analise.

"The lab," she said flatly. "I got into the lab."

Miss Kristian put her arm around Miss Rhona's shoulder and gave her a quick squeeze. "That's the best news!"

Miss Trudia patted her on the back and the other women clucked their approval. Miss Rhona ate what she could, as there were only a few minutes left before the tone sounded, but Miss Kristian noticed the lack of enthusiasm from someone who moments ago said she was starving.

That afternoon, Miss Kristian finished her work cleaning the mechanics' bay and returned to her dorm. The lower bunk next to hers was covered in bedding and a stack of folded clothes was piled on top. Next to those were two kitchen uniforms. On the floor were a colorful empty duffle bag and a pair of dress shoes. She took a peek in the closet and saw unfamiliar dresses hanging from the bar. She showered and went to the lodge for dinner. At the table, she was introduced to her new bunk mate, Miss Chastity.

At day's end, Miss Chastity walked in the women's dorm. The women were eager to talk. Everyone gathered around and sat on the lower bunks except for Miss Trudia, who climbed to the top bunk with Miss Rhona. Miss Chastity said she had been brought in for general kitchen help and to assist in making box lunches for the field workers. Now that the weather was warm, the tractor drivers would be out all day, and with the influx of new boys, more men would be out in the field. They chattered until the tone sounded. The women scrambled to brush their teeth and get in bed. Miss Kristian put on her nightgown and lay down on her lower bunk. Her body ached in loneliness. When the lights were off and she was sure Miss Chastity was asleep, she touched the ball of her foot to the supporting planks of the top bunk. Miss Rhona reached her hand over the side and the two touched fingers.

The two women's disappointment over their new sleeping arrangement was tempered by Miss Chastity's fun personality and the excitement Miss Rhona exuded about her new assignment. Miss Rhona was given a lab coat and felt very professional working side by side with the men. Part of her job, testing pH levels, was a daily necessity. It wasn't a difficult task, and she found it enjoyable to go from tank to tank collecting samples with minimal exposure to the swampy smell. A crew had removed the PlastiCorn panels, leaving the frame behind. Previously, being stationed at the algae tanks all day made her feel like a prisoner behind bars, even when the framing was open. Walking freely through the area gave her a sense of pride and contentment, and greater access to the outdoors stimulated her senses.

Miss Kristian was happy for her friend. The lab work put her in a good mood, some consolation for their lost private time. On several occasions, they managed to hide away in cornfields for hugs and kisses, but they both missed their sleep time together. Miss Kristian had an idea.

"Meet me," she said to Miss Rhona before church.

Miss Rhona looked confused. They could no longer meet for an evening rendezvous of kissing in Miss Kristian's bed with Miss Chastity there.

"After church, after lunch, meet me for a walk."

During services, Miss Kristian turned to the wrong page in

her book and sang the wrong verse. Miss Julie found the right hymn for her, but the words jumped around on the page. She glanced out of the corner of her eye a few seats down to Miss Rhona, who was looking at Miss Trudia, who was looking at a young man across the room.

After lunch was served, Miss Kristian guided Miss Rhona down a road where they laughed about what had happened during the church service. Miss Rhona found Miss Trudia's ogling unseemly.

"Why shouldn't Miss Trudia be interested in a man?" Miss Kristian asked. "Don't you think it's better for two people to fall in love and get married, rather than the Protectorate matching you up with someone you've never met? Look at Mr. and Mrs. Porter. They got married because they loved each other. They're good together. We're meant to be with another person. Plus, I think Miss Julie likes someone, too."

"What's the hurry? We have one to two years left." Miss Rhona sounded annoyed.

"Someday you and I will be matched up—and not to each other. Don't you think it's better to pick someone you like?"

"I'm sorry. I can't...I can't do it. I won't do it!"

"Miss Rhona! Don't say that!"

"Then you tell me—how is it a benefit to all if the Protectorate matches me with a husband I don't want? It's certainly not a benefit to me or you. Where's my protection? This is wrong!"

"You must stop talking like this!"

"That's what they want. They don't want anyone questioning how they do things, otherwise they send you away. I'm not stupid. I may not know what goes on in other countries, but I know there are other ways of doing things. I want to make my own decisions!" Tears burst forth and streamed down Miss Rhona's face. "Don't you see? You're the only one, and I'll never submit to a matched husband. No one here looks at me and that's fine. I don't want a man kissing me. If I can't have you, I won't have anyone!" Miss Rhona exclaimed. She broke away and ran ahead.

"Wait!" Miss Kristian caught up to her. "Come with me. We're almost there. I'm taking you someplace special. In here. Quickly, let's cross the meadow."

Miss Rhona dried her tears. She followed Miss Kristian, who ducked into the copse of aspens and found the marked animal trail. They hastened along for about ten minutes until they came upon the second meadow and stopped. In the distance, they spotted a small herd of deer walking through the flowers, and they watched the graceful animals as they headed into an opening in the forest and disappeared.

"This," Miss Kristian said as she swept her hand across the scene. "This is what I wanted to show you."

"It's beautiful."

"You're beautiful, and I love you."

"And I love you."

They walked hand-in-hand into the meadow and as before, Miss Kristian found flattened out areas where deer had spent the night. They came upon a large area and fell to the ground, kissing passionately. The flowers and grasses had grown high, and they were hidden low to the ground. Carefully, they took off their Sunday clothes and set them aside where they wouldn't become stained. In the light of day, they revealed their nakedness to one another. They touched and kissed, explored and reveled in the instinctual ways of the natural world, expressing their love as if they were married. Their mature bodies rolled together and they gave to the other the sweetness they held in their hearts for so long. The late afternoon sun planted warm kisses along their bodies, mimicking what they did to one another.

"I will always love you," said Miss Kristian, "and you will be in my heart forever." She traced her finger along Miss Rhona's neck, pretending the port wine stain was heart-shaped.

"And I will always love you," Miss Rhona said. "I always have and I always will. You are my love and my life, and somehow, some day, I will find a way for us to be together—forever."

They sealed their vows with long kisses and planned to return to the meadow as often as they could. "Meet me" took on a whole new meaning.

Chapter Five

A n early summer assembly was called with invitations to parents. Mr. Browne came in for the event. He hugged his daughter and his eyes looked glassy when he released her. They spent the day together and of course included Miss Rhona. After lunch, Miss Kristian took him to the mechanics' shed and then Miss Rhona showed him where she worked.

"You aren't girls anymore," he said as Miss Rhona gave him a tour of the lab.

"No, sir. I'm doing real work now. In fact, I'm putting in some time on my own research study. I have to do it in my free time, and there's not much of that. Still, I think I can make important contributions while I'm here."

Mr. Browne gave her a hug. "I'm very proud of you, Miss Rhona. You're like another daughter to me. I hope you'll remember me when you have children. It never hurts to have another grandfather."

"Thank you, Mr. Browne. I'll remember you said that."

"Now, if you'll excuse us, my daughter and I need to meet another potential set of grandparents."

Miss Rhona shot her friend a questioning look and Miss Kristian raised her eyebrows, silently shrugging her shoulders in reply as her father led her off. They returned to the lodge. Sitting inside by the large stone fireplace was Mr. Stewart. He rose when he saw Miss Kristian, greeted her, and motioned for her to join him.

Zoe Amos

"Father, this is my friend, Mr. Stewart. We worked together for a while in the mechanics' shed."

"My pleasure." Mr. Browne extended his hand.

Mr. Stewart turned and called to a man standing several feet away. "Father!" The man walked over. "Father, this is the Mr. Browne I told you about." They shook hands. "And his daughter, Miss Kristian."

"Hello, sir," Miss Kristian said. "Nice to meet you."

"My, you are tall! My son wasn't kidding. A real beauty, too. Now, where did Mrs. Stewart run off to at an important time like this?"

Miss Kristian felt anxiety rise within her as she realized this was not a chance meeting. Mr. Stewart was making plans for her to be his wife and now she was meeting his family. His mother joined them and the five of them sat together getting acquainted.

The elder Mr. Stewart spoke of his large tract, modestly revealing a successful operation extending many years back. He listened intently as Mr. Browne explained his position at the feed mill. Mr. Stewart did not seem bothered by their disparity in standing. It would have been more likely to matter had his daughter been looking for a husband, and not the other way around.

Mrs. Stewart's pearl dangle earrings swayed as she nodded from time to time during conversation. She wore a heavy link bracelet accented with a round gold emblem carved in a floral design. Miss Kristian asked about it and she opened it to reveal a watch. Mrs. Stewart talked about her family as treasures in their own way, saving the strongest complements for her son, whose eyes rarely strayed from Miss Kristian.

They concluded their visit with Mr. Browne agreeing for his daughter to see the Stewart tract later that summer. Except when answering questions, Miss Kristian was speechless. It would have been out of turn for her to say anything contrary, and there was nothing she could say. As a potential husband, Mr. Stewart was a good catch. It didn't hurt that he was handsome. Any woman in their right mind would be thrilled. Before he left, Mr. Browne had a few private words with Mr. and Mrs. Porter. Miss Kristian bade good-bye to her father, returned to her room and cried.

Chapter Six

Each day, Miss Rhona logged algae pH readings. Once the spring rainy season was over, rainfall was scarce. While the algae could thrive with a certain amount of gray water, it was important to replenish it with fresh water diverted from the reservoirs. When the algae had grown to its maximum potential in the tank, it was harvested, the tank was drained, and the process started over again. The fetid water was blended with fresh to increase the oxygen level before it was used for crop irrigation. When the tank was refilled, she noted the new pH level. Rainfall made the pH levels fluctuate depending on the amount, and this was normal. She found the work interesting and useful.

Blue-green alga was needed for food. Other kinds were used to make biofuel. More experienced men in the lab supervised the production. When she had time, Miss Rhona studied the pH charts and played around with small samples in the biofuel lab. She seemed invisible to the other men who stayed focused on their work. Her new assignment brought a sense of fulfillment and she fantasized about staying in the lab beyond her marrying year. Perhaps a job well done would please the Protectorate and give them a reason to make an exception. Likewise, Miss Kristian could mentor a new batch of girls, thus allowing the two to stay together.

Guided by the scheduled times on her roster, Miss Rhona made the rounds to various tanks. She kneeled down to fill small tubes with murky water for testing. As she collected her samples, she heard someone walking. His shoes stopped near her and she looked up. It was Mr. Kowalski.

"What are you doing here? Women shouldn't be playing with food. You should be in the kitchen," he said with a smirk, "cooking it."

She rolled her eyes. "I'm taking pH samples."

"How do I know you aren't adding poison?"

"Such a thought!" Miss Rhona was horrified. "Where do you get these ideas?"

Mr. Kowalski frowned as he looked down on her. "If I had my way, women would be removed from the face of this planet, especially women like you. I'd better not see you here again." As he left, he knocked over her samples, spilling their contents.

She waited until he left and then hastened to redo her work. She was considerably upset, not so much at the minor annoyance Mr. Kowalski had created by adding to her work, but at his unspecified threat. As a preemptive strike, she returned to the lab and mentioned the "accident" to her supervisor, who assured her by saying Mr. Kowalski had other problems and not to take it personally.

Later, when she and Miss Kristian were walking back to their dorm after dinner, she recounted the event. In the retelling, it seemed trifling and Miss Kristian thought it best to forget the incident. As they approached the dorm, they heard loud noises, arguing, and crying. They ran to see about the commotion. A few of their dorm mates were standing in the common area. Their eyes were red and watery. Miss Trudia was crying in her room while Mrs. Porter gathered her clothes.

"Let me marry him! Tonight! I'll marry him tonight!" Miss Trudia wailed.

"I'm sorry, Miss Trudia. You're not of marrying age. We can't do it."

"But he's already put in his request! You know we want to marry!"

"What's going on here?" Miss Kristian asked the others.

Miss Julie placed her hand over her tummy and made a rounded motion.

"Miss Kristian!" Miss Trudia's stare dug into Miss Kristian with renewed hope. "You're strong. Stop her! He wants to marry me! Tell her to let us get married. Don't let them take my baby!"

Miss Kristian stood silent with her mouth agape.

Mrs. Porter closed the suitcase. "There's nothing Miss Kristian or anyone else can do for you now. After you have the baby, your request case will be discussed. Be glad you'll be helping a less fortunate family realize their dreams." Mrs. Porter gripped the handle of the bag with one hand, grasped Miss Trudia's wrist with her other and marched toward the door. Miss Trudia was weak from hysterics and followed reluctantly, stumbling over her own feet.

"Sorry you girls have to see this." Mrs. Porter sighed. "Immature decisions by immature couples are not rewarded. Let this be a lesson to you all."

Mr. Harlingen appeared at the front door and took the bag from Mrs. Porter. The three of them walked to a waiting vehicle. He tossed her bag into the rear compartment and Miss Trudia fell to her knees in heaving sobs. Mrs. Porter helped her up. She brushed off Miss Trudia's dress and using her own apron wiped tears from Miss Trudia's face. She held Miss Trudia, and when the young woman's sobs died down, helped her into the back seat. Mr. Harlingen closed the door, got in the passenger seat, and the driver pulled away.

Chapter Seven

M iss Trudia's expulsion cast a pall over the farm camp for a few days, resulting in hushed voices at meal times. The workers listened to a church sermon that seemed hastily put together about the Garden of Eden. Adam and Eve were cast out—banished—a punishment worse than plagues.

"The Protectorate is a union of sorts," the minister said, "like a marriage between everyone who lives in the great land of Superior, and we would all be well-advised to adhere to the rules for the benefit of all. So be it."

Miss Kristian wondered if Mr. Harlingen would call assembly, but he did not. What would have been the point? Everyone knew. The men carried on, including Miss Trudia's potential fiancé. Grieving showed on his face and in his step. He lost his girlfriend and their child, punishment enough. The women in the dorm understood the consequences. And when Miss Julie walked with her beau, they kept their hands to themselves.

The incident made it easier for Miss Kristian to be friends with Mr. Stewart without concern of unwanted overtures. Mr. Stewart found reason to come to the mechanics' shed and came by for the sake of greetings alone. These were short visits, sprinkled with niceties. He asked to see her during quiet time after dinner, as there were things he needed to discuss.

"It sure is wonderful having extra daylight," he said when they met after dinner. "The equinox is only weeks away." Miss Kristian nodded. He suggested they take a stroll and they walked to the edge of the cornfields. "These warm evenings are my favorite time. Soon, it'll be too hot and muggy."

"It's already buggy."

"Our family home has a screened porch; no slapping mosquitoes all night."

"Sounds nice."

"I've made plans for your visit. You'll have your own room and you won't have to work while you're there. I've seen to that."

"I don't mind working. I pull my weight."

"This time you're a guest, but bring your overalls anyway. My parents are excited you're coming and everyone else is looking forward to meeting you."

"When are we going?" asked Miss Kristian.

"Next week. Mrs. Porter knows you'll be leaving with me. My father will send a driver for us."

Miss Kristian nodded her assent. She had never been a guest in another person's home and wondered what she would do all day with no work detail. She went back to the dorm to tell Miss Rhona and Miss Chastity, who were already getting ready for sleep. Miss Chastity stepped out to brush her teeth and Miss Rhona shut the door.

"You shouldn't go. You have to find a way out," Miss Rhona said when Miss Chastity was out of earshot.

"I don't make these decisions."

"Don't you see? You're being led. The next thing you know, he'll put in a request for you. Your father will be thrilled."

Miss Kristian noted the chill in Miss Rhona's voice. "This is the world we live in," she replied. "What do you expect me to do about it? Do you think I should attempt something stupid like trying to swim the Straits of Mackinaw? They wouldn't even come after me. The current would take me away and they'd watch me drown."

Miss Rhona covered her face with her hands. "Stop! I have to think!" She pressed her hands together in front of her as if she were in prayer, and tapped the sides of her index fingers to her mouth. "I will think of something."

The following week, Miss Kristian didn't see much of Miss Rhona, who spent most of her free time in the lab. Miss Kristian didn't want to ask if she was hatching a plan of some sort. It was apparent she had thrown herself into her work. At this rate, not only would they never be able to spend their lives together, no one would request Miss Rhona and the Protectorate would match her up with another single with no prospects.

At the appointed time for her travel, Miss Kristian waited with Mr. Stewart in the lodge with her packed bag. The morning rain abated and the sun dried the landscape. When their driver arrived, he ushered them into the back seat, stowed their bags and drove off. Passing beneath the high arches of pleaching trees transported her in a magical way, previewing a new life of privilege. She wasn't taken to other locations often, and the sights along the highway, however banal to an experienced traveler, elicited wonder and curiosity about the world in which she lived. She and Mr. Stewart commented on the sights as they passed through forests, the northern frontage of Lake Michigan, the bustling city of Manistique and beyond. Eventually, she settled into the comfort of her seat. The long drive became tiresome and she was glad when Mr. Stewart noted landmarks as they approached their final destination near Sault Saint Marie.

The driver stopped before a gated entrance. Miss Kristian forced open her droopy lids and made an effort to rouse herself. They pulled into a circular driveway. Mrs. Stewart greeted them with hugs and the driver took their bags inside the manse.

"What a beautiful entry," Miss Kristian said.

"Thank you," said Mrs. Stewart. "I'm sure you're tired. Why don't we save the tour for later, after you've had a chance to rest? I'll take you to your room."

They walked through a lobby and went up a long curved stairway with polished wood banisters. They passed several open doors, each revealing a beautifully decorated bedroom.

"These bedrooms look unused. Who are they for?"

"This is the guest wing. We live in another part of the house. Here." Mrs. Stewart brought her into a larger room at the end of the hall. "We don't have other company right now, so I gave you the master suite. Everything you need should be here, but if we've forgotten anything, do let us know."

A king-sized poster bed was against one wall. Pillows lined the back and a light-weight comforter was already turned down. Matching side tables and a dresser lined the walls and yet there was plenty of room to walk. There were two more doors inside the room. Miss Kristian walked toward one. "May I see?"

Mrs. Steward nodded.

Miss Kristian opened the door and walked in. "It's a closet! As big as my dorm room. Is this a closet, too?" She walked to the other door and peeked inside.

"No, dear. It's the bathroom. We've laid out towels and toiletries for you."

"These are for me?" Miss Kristian looked stunned.

"Yes. Come downstairs when you're ready, or I'll send up someone to let you know when to expect dinner." Mrs. Stewart excused herself, closing the door on her way out.

Miss Kristian walked into the bathroom. The countertops were polished granite, as were the two sinks. The shower stall had large granite tiles on three sides. She recognized the shower head for what it was, but the faucet controls were unfamiliar and looked complicated. The toilet was set off to one side and had a pocket door for privacy. She held the towels to her face and breathed in a light floral scent. They were so thick, she imagined a hand towel would suffice to dry her entire body. She splashed water on her face and patted it dry. The bed sat much higher off the ground than any in which she had ever slept. Not wanting to crush the beautiful pillow, she lay down on the bed sideways and fell asleep.

She woke to light tapping on her door. A woman entered and introduced herself as Miss Lilah. She helped Miss Kristian with the shower adjustments, and then again after Miss Kristian toweled off, by brushing and braiding her long blonde hair. She escorted her to the dining area where Mr. Stewart's sister, Miss Bettina was already seated.

An older woman helped Miss Lilah serve dinner. Miss Kristian watched the Stewart family for cues on how to behave. She had never been served individually, been offered choice pieces of food, or had her dishes removed with such elegance. Mr. Stewart's parents spoke about farm business with their son. Miss Kristian spoke when spoken to, as did Miss Bettina. After the meal, she and Mr. Stewart sat on the screened porch and talked awhile. Miss Bettina butted in, insisting Miss Kristian look at her doll collection before they retired for the night.

The sun rose earlier on the eastern end of the Protectorate and Miss Kristian lay awake in bed as the dawn light streamed through a crack in the drapery. She thought about the delicious food she had been served and could hardly wait for breakfast, except for the fact her bed was amazingly comfortable. She fingered the fine linen, marveling at its smoothness and detail. Her father lived in meager surroundings. His job did not provide for much, and while he was given food, clothing and shelter, he had to fill out requisition forms for other basic necessities. Why, she questioned, did the Protectorate allow some families to scrape by while others lived in abundance?

Breakfast was a dream. Miss Lilah was willing to prepare anything Miss Kristian requested. Not wanting to cause a fuss, she asked for whatever Miss Bettina would be having and was pleasantly surprised with a plate of blueberry waffles, genuine maple syrup, bacon, and fresh cherries. She ate with the family minus the elder Mr. Stewart. When Mrs. Stewart left, Miss Bettina followed and she was left alone with her friend.

"I hope you like it here," he said.

"It's amazing! I didn't know there were houses like this. Yesterday, when we drove up, I thought it was a hotel. If I were here, I'd never want to leave. Why are you at the Escanaba farm camp when you have this?"

"Politics." He saw the confusion on Miss Kristian's face. "Families like mine helped the Protectorate get established. Taking our property would have extended the war. They needed our support and in return we put on a good front. Anyway, I'm glad I went to the farm camp or I never would have met you! Come on. I'll give you a tour of the grounds."

His first stop was at the kennel where he showed her their two dogs. He took her around the property and pointed out silos, barns, warehouses, and farm housing for the workers. Men were out in the fields and others were at work around the property busy with a variety of farm duties. Their last stop was the elder Mr. Stewart's office. After a brief chat, the younger Mr. Stewart asked permission to take Miss Kristian out for a tractor ride and his father agreed.

They returned to the house for another delicious meal. Afterward, Mr. Stewart suggested Miss Kristian change her clothes. She put on her overalls and he took her to a tractor housed in a barn.

"I told you I'd show you how to drive one of these things. Now's your chance."

He showed her where to step, and gripping the rails, she hoisted herself up. Mr. Stewart climbed in the other side.

"Are you sure you don't want to drive and I can watch?" she asked.

"I'm sure. This is how I learned and you can, too."

He spent time going over the functions of the various levers and pedals. Before she would have guessed, she had the behemoth in gear and lurching toward a field. Power steering made maneuvering easy, but it still took strength to corner and she misjudged her turns. Mr. Stewart laughed and she laughed with him. She gave it another try and stayed on the road. Steering wasn't too hard by itself, but steering while working the gears was tricky. An hour was all she could take. Mr. Stewart drove them back to their starting point.

At the house she heard a piano. They followed the melody to the music room where his sister was having a lesson. Miss Kristian asked to stay and sat in a chair on the far end of the room while Miss Bettina did finger exercises.

In the late afternoon, Miss Kristian changed into her dress and sat inside the screened porch. Miss Lilah brought out iced tea and little cakes that Miss Kristian could have devoured with one bite. She watched Mrs. Stewart nibble a corner and she did the same. They talked about their different lives. Mrs. Stewart shared some reading materials that she then left for Miss Kristian to take to her room.

The following day was filled with more activities Miss Kristian could not have imagined. She went with Miss Bettina to a room set up with an easel and paints. Miss Bettina had started a picture of a vase with flowers. She set up a thick piece of paper for Miss Kristian and showed her how to mix water with the paint and apply the brush to the paper. Miss Kristian had never fancied herself an artist; however, she enjoyed the activity.

In the afternoon, Mr. Stewart offered another driving lesson, which Miss Kristian thought to decline until he told her it was on an old ATV, an all-terrain vehicle that would take them to the far reaches of the property. He fitted her with a helmet and donned one himself. He sat up front and instructed her to put her arms around his waist and hold on. It was embarrassing to hold him, and she was glad he couldn't see her flush. He drove off slowly down a dirt road. After a while he picked up speed and Miss Kristian held on with all her might. At the rise of a hill, he stopped. She was not used to the vibration from the vehicle and was glad for the break.

He walked a short way to a family plot and she followed behind at a respectful distance. There were several markers on the ground. He knelt and said a prayer over one of them.

"My older brother," he said. "He died suddenly a few years ago."

"Oh, I'm sorry."

"See that over there?" he said, pointing northward. "Those are the Soo Locks. As you know, freighters coming across Lake Superior have to go through the St. Mary's River to get to Lake Huron. There's a marked drop in elevation, and the locks raise and lower the ships so they can get from one lake to the other. That's Canada in the distance. You can't see it from here, but there's a trench and a wall to keep us protected from them."

"Is it scary to live this close to the border?"

"No. They don't care about us anymore. We're just a small country. Canada is huge! They have everything they need. Our treaties keep the locks open and dictate our water rights, but otherwise, I don't know if I would trust them. Some of the people there speak different languages. You can own a gun and have as many dogs as you want. Cars are everywhere. Women marry women and men marry men. It's wild and dangerous!"

"What?!"

"It's true, Miss Kristian. Polar bears and wolves roam the streets. It's beyond bizarre—it's pure mayhem! Be glad you're here and not there."

Mr. Stewart took out a bag of cherries and offered her some. As she ate, Miss Kristian gazed at the large city across the border, noting its many inlets. Ships inched along the waterway. She wondered if what he said was true. Could women really marry women? She chewed slowly on the sweet red fruit, and fantasized how she and Miss Rhona might steal across the border.

Mr. Stewart put Miss Kristian in front for the ride back. He showed her how to change gears by clicking a pedal down with her foot. She caught on quickly and thrilled to feel the air racing past her skin. He showed her how to turn a corner safely and to mount a rise so the ATV wouldn't tip over. She pulled into the barn and they dismounted. While he went for a canister of fuel, she looked at the engine.

"This would be fun to take apart and put back together," she said when he returned.

"Well, if you want to do that, I won't stop you," he said. "This engine was made for gasoline, not an ethanol/biofuel mix. It could use some tinkering."

"We did a conversion once on a van engine at my boarding school."

"And you can do one here, too. You'll have plenty of time for that after you're my wife. In case you haven't guessed, I'm putting in a request with the Protectorate for you."

"I thought you might."

The next day, Miss Kristian was very happy to see her dorm mates at the farm camp. She shared the soaps Mrs. Stewart gave her so the sisterhood could enjoy their pleasant feel and flowery scents. When she had a moment in private with Miss Rhona, they silently embraced and kissed for a long time.

"I missed you," Miss Kristian said.

"Did you? You made it sound like you couldn't wait to be the new Mrs. Stewart, living a life of luxury. Life on the Stewart tract—paint all morning, take apart engines all afternoon, eat gourmet cooking. What could be better?"

"Please, Miss Rhona. Jealousy doesn't become you."

"Jealousy! You think I'm jealous? The last thing I want is to be some rich man's wife, or any man's wife. Have you forgotten our vows?"

"No." Miss Kristian paused. She held Miss Rhona's face in her hands. "I love you—only you! I mean it. I had an idea. Remember I told you about Miss Lilah? She's not very old. Something must have happened, like maybe what happened with Miss Trudia. She's never been married and she's definitely past marrying age. I could try to find out how she ended up working there. Maybe you could work there, too."

Miss Rhona's petite body crumpled at the suggestion. "Don't you understand? I can't work for you. I couldn't bear to see you everyday with him, being with him, having his children. I'd rather be dead!" A tear ran down her face.

"Don't cry." Miss Kristian rocked her. "I'm trying to find a way for us to be together, that's all. I don't suppose you've come up with anything better?"

"No."

"I have something to tell you. Mr. Stewart says in Canada women marry other women."

"How does that help us?"

"Miss Rhona, please listen to me. We have to get to Canada."

Chapter Eight

The next morning, Miss Kristian was assigned cleaning duty for the corn pickers. The early corn was already being harvested and put on the table. The kernels were small, sweet, and succulent. She loved early corn barely cooked and served hot with alga oil mixed with butter. Cleaning corn pickers did not require much concentration and thinking about the goodness of corn seemed a natural place for her mind to wander. Figuring out how she and Miss Rhona would get to Canada seemed impossible.

Tall corn stalks meant she and Miss Rhona could sneak away without being seen. "Meet me" became a recurring refrain. After church, the two women tore through the secret path and made love in the open air. Deer would amble by, unconcerned about the noises coming from the meadow, and red-winged blackbirds would cry out their distinctive call. As they lay naked together one afternoon, a beautiful bird song filled the meadow, a haunting repetition in a minor key.

"I know that bird," said Miss Rhona. "It's a white-throated sparrow. Its song is said to be one of the most beautiful in nature."

"You're my white-throated sparrow," said Miss Kristian as she kissed Miss Rhona's neck.

Miss Rhona laughed. "Red-winged blackbirds like water. I bet there's a pond near here. Let's look."

The two dressed and set out to explore across the far end of the meadow. At the edge of the forest they looked for anything resembling a trail. They spied an opening and Miss Kristian marked their spot by breaking a branch. She continued to mark their trail as they continued on. The forest here was mostly spruce and pine. The underbrush was less dense and the forest floor was soft with pine needles. Squirrels scampered away and climbed tree trunks as the two walked down a shallow ravine.

"Listen! Do you hear it?" Miss Rhona asked. "Running water." She pointed at a thin stream of water trickling through a cleft in the earth. "There's the pond."

They walked a short distance downhill. The pond was thick with cattails. Birds alit on the rushes and flitted from stalk to stalk.

"Oh, my! Look at that!" Miss Kristian said. "A cabin. Or what's left of it."

"No one's lived here in a long time. It's barely standing."

They ventured toward the one-room cabin. Its windows were gone and what was left of the roof had turned into a garden of grass and flowers. Black-eyed Susan, a daisy-like flower with yellow petals and a dark center, sprang up in comical fashion from the matted roof. Making their way through the undergrowth, they peered inside the cabin. An old battered woodstove was the most recognizable feature. They identified a bed frame by the few rusty springs resting on the weedy floor. Bent rusted cans were strewn around the open space. Miss Kristian walked past the missing doorway and saw something hidden by brush.

"Miss Rhona! Look at this!"

Miss Rhona quickly came around the corner. "What is it? A buried motorcycle?"

"I think it's a snowmobile, like the one Mr. Porter used to have. Remember the photo he showed us during the first assembly?"

"Honestly, no."

"I remember. I remember anything with an engine."

"Well, this pile of rust is beyond repair. I know you're fascinated, but we should get back before someone starts looking for us."

Miss Kristian agreed this was true. As they left, she looked over her shoulder knowing she would return.

During the week, Miss Kristian was intent on learning more about the cabin and what might be found there, but Miss Rhona had more pressing issues on her mind.

"Have you noticed anything unusual this year about the weather?" she asked Miss Kristian. "Does it seem cooler?"

"Now that you mention it. I guess I've been enjoying the mild days before we get the full heat of summer."

"And have you noticed it's been a little rainy?"

"Yes. That's a good thing. We've been able to conserve our resources. Why?"

"I record pH levels in the algae tanks and I'm seeing a pattern I don't like. Since you left on your trip I've been capturing rainfall. I've tested the pH and it has a high acid content, higher than usual."

"Is that bad?"

"It's good that you're using less water to irrigate. The rain isn't acidic enough to hurt the plants, but we've had to correct the pH in our algae tanks by adding neutralizers. I brought it to the attention of my supervisor. I suggested reinstalling the overhead panels to cover the tanks. There are two reasons. First, it will heat the air underneath and bring the algae growth up to normal for this time of year. It will also keep the rain from infiltrating our tanks and disturbing the pH levels."

"You amaze me. You are so brilliant!"

"That's what my supervisor said. The panels should go up tomorrow."

The next day, Miss Rhona stayed out of the workers' way as they installed the PlastiCorn panels. Drainage alternatives hadn't been considered, but there was no time for elaborate changes to the basic setup. Mr. Kowalski was there passing dingy panes to a worker on a ladder. She left before he could see her.

That night it rained and washed the panels clean. The next day, Miss Rhona checked the pH levels in the pond and in a few rain gauges she had set up elsewhere. Her plan was effective in reducing the total amount of rainwater entering the algae tanks. The rain collected from the gauges showed a progressive rise in acid. But why? This new problem worried her. On her own, she decided to chart the air temperature. It was off by about 2.7 degrees from the previous year, not a statistically significant amount for a short-term measurement. Winter temperatures had been normal and it was merely a cool spring. The temperature in the algae tanks would rise with the advancing season. She guessed it would not take long for the pools to warm, especially with clean panels in place.

In a matter of days, the tanks warmed. Her suggestion had been a success on both counts. They were able to maintain the pH levels using fewer additives, and the algae growth would now bloom normally. She discussed her findings at the dinner meal with her dorm mates, who were very impressed.

"Smart people like you make the Protectorate a better place," said Miss Chastity as she dug into her dessert, cornbread with a light honey drizzle.

Miss Rhona smiled. "Thank you. You're very kind. I wish I could be in the lab forever. And I'm enjoying your contribution. This cornbread is delicious."

"Thanks! I hope my children enjoy my cooking some day as much as all of you."

The women finished their meal and when they got up to leave, Mrs. Porter asked Miss Rhona to stay. "Why don't you stay, too?" she asked Miss Kristian. They continued to chat as the dining area cleared out. "Let's talk a walk," she said.

She moseyed onto a mowed green area, waddling side-to-side with her body weight shifting with each step. She sat on the edge of a picnic table bench and the two took places on the opposite side.

"I have something on my mind," Mrs. Porter said. "You two have been an important part of our success here at the Escanaba farm camp. Miss Rhona, your supervisor told me about your contributions before you shared with us this evening. I'm very proud of you. And Miss Kristian, I know you are doing a wonderful job. It's important to have interests as part of being well-rounded women."

Miss Kristian smiled and Miss Rhona tried not to appear smug. It would be wonderful if Mrs. Porter pulled strings to allow Miss Rhona to stay on at the lab.

"You two are very close. I know you've been friends for many years."

"Miss Kristian is like a sister to me," said Miss Rhona. "I couldn't ask for a better friend."

Mrs. Porter looked stern. "Miss Kristian, you know Mr. Stewart has requested you."

"Yes, I know."

"And you will be marrying him. You'll go with him and live on his tract, right?"

Miss Kristian remained silent for a few seconds longer than she thought prudent and blurted out her reply. "Yes. He's been very kind." She glanced at Miss Rhona, who appeared serious.

"Sometimes," Mrs. Porter said, "how shall I say this, two women form an attachment—an unhealthy attachment. Maybe they haven't had an opportunity to appreciate what a young man can bring to their lives, and instead of coupling with a man, they choose one another."

Miss Kristian dared not take a breath. She clenched her teeth and her eyes widened. This wasn't the direction she hoped the conversation would take. She noticed the muscles standing out in Miss Rhona's neck.

"I've seen this happen," she continued. "Those women get sent away—not as a couple. They will never see one another again." She paused. The women said nothing. "Married women, particularly ones with means, have occasion to travel around the Protectorate. They have help in the home, and can visit friends and family."

"Mr. Stewart's family has a woman who lives with them, Miss Lilah. Where did she come from? Is she one of those women you're talking about?"

"I don't know Miss Lilah. I thought you two might need to hear what I have to say. As your keeper, I care about you. You've been entrusted in my care for most of a year. I want good things for you both."

"Yes, Mrs. Porter. We both appreciate everything you've done for us," Miss Kristian said.

"Yes," said Miss Rhona.

"There's one other thing," Mrs. Porter said as she looked at Miss Rhona. "Women aren't the only ones who make these attachments. Men do, too. I've heard of cases where these men have been introduced to women who don't seem to be able to connect with the other men they've met. I could look into this."

Miss Rhona swallowed hard.

"It can be a workable situation that evolves into caring and love. The Superior Fertility Department may even prescribe treatment so the couple can have a family. I thought you should know."

Miss Rhona nodded. Her lips were sealed firmly together and her chin trembled. Mrs. Porter pushed off the table top to stand. "I'll expect to see you two back at the dorm room shortly."

When she rounded the corner of the lodge and was out of sight, Miss Rhona put her head down on the picnic table. "Please tell me this isn't happening. Please tell me this isn't my life! Tell me I'm dreaming and I'll wake up in your arms." She began to cry softly.

Miss Kristian put her arm around her and then thought better of it. Had someone already seen them together?

"She's giving us fair warning about what she knows, or she thinks she knows. Miss Rhona, she's telling you, telling us, our options. If you don't meet a man, the Protectorate will match you up with someone who will want you to behave like a wife. I think she's empathetic to who we are and what we feel. She would make an introduction for you to a man who wouldn't expect anything, and you and I could visit from time to time. Otherwise, we may end up as a nanny like Miss Lilah with no real family of our own and no chance to see one another. Maybe we would be banished and never heard from again!"

"These are choices? These are nothing! My life is nothing without you, and if you can't see that, maybe you should go with Mr. Stewart and forget about me!"

Miss Rhona wiped her eyes on her sleeve, got up from the table and left without looking back. Miss Kristian was tempted to run after her. Her eyes flooded and tears splashed down onto the table.

The persistent chill in the outside air extended into the dorm room where Miss Kristian and Miss Rhona were politely distant. Miss Kristian lay in bed with the lights off. Her winter covers, which she should have shed by this time, were cocooned around her shoulders. She felt empty and remembered the days before

Miss Chastity arrived, when the two would snuggle in her lower bunk as naturally as two foxes in a den. Cold, damp weather made her long for warmth, but there was none to be had, not in her bed and not in the arms of her lover.

Miss Rhona became engrossed in her lab work. She came in for dinner when the tone sounded, prayed and ate with the others, and then returned to the lab. With no special "meet me" agenda in the offing, Miss Kristian wandered the grounds or as often as not, headed back to the dorm for chats with the sisterhood. An edgy restlessness made her feel like moving around, yet sadness left her limbs heavy and unwilling to trudge to the old cabin where she had wanted to explore further. Once, she went to the lab out of curiosity. She peered in the window and watched unobserved as Miss Rhona engaged in a long conversation with her supervisor as they took turns at a microscope.

Unrelenting cold mist was not good for the corn and Miss Kristian became concerned about the crop. Bacteria, mold, and fungus could damage the ears. Surely the sun would come out full force any day for the hot, dry season. Everyone spoke of it.

At dinner, wanting to initiate better communication, she brought Miss Rhona an ear of corn on the pretext the husk was showing black mold.

"Some men are already looking into it," Miss Rhona said crisply.

Miss Kristian sighed.

When the meal ended and the women got up to leave, Miss Rhona whispered into Miss Kristian's ear, "Wait." Miss Kristian dropped a fork and Miss Rhona offered to retrieve it from beneath the table. They stalled until the others left. Miss Kristian looked at her, wanting to know what was going on. "Let's walk," Miss Rhona said.

They ventured out onto the dirt road and Miss Kristian wondered if Miss Rhona was thinking they would go to their special place. It seemed unlikely.

"I have something to tell you," Miss Rhona said. "It's about what's going on in the lab."

"Have you made a discovery?"

"Yes. There's a problem in the atmosphere. You can't see it, but you can feel it in the cold and rain. Usually, it's much drier and the tractors send up clouds of dust. The dirt lands on everything and the PlastiCorn panels over the algae tanks get covered. This misty rain is keeping the dust level down, but I saw a film covering the panels and decided to check it out. There are high concentrations of particulates in the air. They give high level moisture something to form around—a seed for a raindrop. That's why we're getting all this rain and that's why it's cooler. There are so many particulates it's changing the weather."

Miss Kristian considered this. "Why? What's causing it?"

Miss Rhona stopped walking. "It's ash."

"From a forest fire?"

"No. From a volcano."

"A volcano? That's impossible! There aren't any volcanoes around here."

"That's true, so wherever this ash is coming from, it drifted from far away. The ash is a superfine particle that gets swept into the upper atmosphere. The volcano could be in the western United States or another country across the ocean. We have no way of knowing because the Protectorate isn't saying. We know about it here at the Escanaba farm camp, so I'm sure they know."

Miss Kristian tented her fingers over her mouth and dropped her hand over her throat. "Oh, no! How bad is it?"

"Eruptions can start out strong and just as quickly die out, or volcanoes can send out blasts for weeks or months. Somewhere in the world, there's been an eruption and we're in the stream of the fallout—at least we're getting some of it. It could be worse elsewhere. This isn't the first time in history something like this has happened. We've been having a problem adjusting the acid/alkaline mix in the algae tanks. It's also getting into the earth and we may have to correct the soil. You see, when ash mixes with rain, it creates acid rain. It's not good, and if the level of ash increases, we may have to wear masks."

"That's awful! Is it safe to be outside?"

"For your own protection, you should stay indoors as much as possible. If this keeps up, we could have a very cold winter. Mr. Harlingen should be calling for an assembly soon. You can't say anything. Promise?"

"Yes, I promise. Thank you for confiding in me." She restrained her urge to hug her friend.

"Let's go back to the dorm."

For the next few days, Miss Kristian worked in the mechanics' bays and tried not to venture outside any more than necessary. There was no assembly called and she questioned the veracity of Miss Rhona's claims. Surely the Protectorate would ensure their safety. On clear days, she looked for evidence in the sky and saw nothing, but when she ran her finger along random surfaces, her fingertip was coated with fine gray-brown dust. There was no way for her to know if it was dirt from the farm or if some of it was fine ash from a distant volcano.

The succeeding days cleared and the farm dried out with the help of the warming northern sun with its long daylight hours. Eruptions could start and they could stop. Summer arrived late and it was welcomed by everyone tired of the cold, rainy weather. The sisterhood stored their extra blankets and put away their flannel nightgowns.

Brighter days picked up Miss Kristian's mood. With Miss Rhona in the lab every night and the landscape drying out, she decided to indulge her curiosity about the old cabin. After dinner, she changed into her overalls and tromped through the forest. Rabbits scattered to all sides as she passed through the meadow on the way. The creek was still running and she made her way down the small hill to the pond.

Upon closer examination of the cabin, she saw what looked to be the remains of a waterwheel. The pond, smaller from years of dry weather, was now about twenty feet from the cabin. She imagined what it might have looked like with a roiling stream turning the waterwheel. Inside the dilapidated structure, she found rusted pieces of metal and had no idea as to their former purpose. Brown, green, and clear glass bottles were strewn about. She held up a couple filled with varying levels of dirt and imagined their former contents.

Outside, she looked at the old snowmobile. She dug at the ground with her heel, but realized her efforts would be fruitless. She found a few items as she wandered around, a wood handle with no tool attached, the rim of a rusted out enamel tub, and the edges of a thick plastic bucket.

Aspens had grown up around the cabin. She walked along an open area and noticed another kind of tree planted in rows. Upon closer inspection, the grizzled limbs held greenish-brown misshapen fruit about the size of a baby potato. She picked one and gouged her fingernail into the flesh. It was juicy and smelled of apple. Touching her tongue to the exposed fruit, she was delightfully surprised with its flavor. She peeled the mottled skin away and nibbled at the wonderful sweetness before tossing the core to the ground. She picked another with fewer blemishes, tucked it into her bib and decided to go.

On the way back, she spotted a flattened shed peeking out from beneath a cover of ferns. The roof was gone and the side boards curled. She kicked up on the corner of a thick board and lifted it with her hands. It was heavy with dirt and didn't pry up easily. Giving it an extra pull, the board splintered and revealed a trove of tools in surprisingly good condition. She gasped at her discovery and pulled at the remaining splintered end, being careful not to hurt herself. This allowed her easier access to the adjacent board and she removed that one, too. She pulled out several usable items, shovels, hoes, and more, and laid them in a neat row. It was impossible to see what else might be beneath the boards and she didn't have the time to find out. She looked at the shovel and knew what she must do. As she was leaving, she leaned the handle against the snowmobile and walked back to the dorm, eager to return. But first, she had to find Mr. Porter.

Chapter Nine

The next day after Sunday services, Miss Rhona, in preparation for work in the lab, returned to the dorm to wash up. She greeted Miss Analise.

"Mr. Stewart went for a walk with Miss Kristian," Miss Analise said. "You two aren't as close as you used to be. Do you want to talk about it?"

Miss Rhona shrugged. "What's there to say? People change. We'll all be moving on eventually."

"I could introduce you to a nice man—my older brother. A long time ago he was sweet on someone, but he's kind of shy. He didn't act soon enough and she married someone else. Instead of finding another woman or asking for a match, he threw himself into his work. To be honest, he's eleven years older. I think he's lonely and you seem lonely."

Miss Rhona smiled. "I don't know. I'm pretty happy with my work."

"You can't do that forever. You're a good, caring person, and smart, and so is he. He has a good position in the Oncology Department at Superior City Medical Center. They're letting him specialize and he's already doing well. I think you two have a lot in common. At some point, the Protectorate is bound to push him to find a mate. You two could be a good match. Perhaps he could arrange for you to see someone in Dermatology to do something about..." she touched her own neck instead of Miss Rhona's, "that is, if it bothers you. I'm sure it wouldn't bother him. I think he would like you as his wife."

"You're very kind to be thinking of me and my future, Miss Analise. I'll let you know."

Miss Rhona hustled off to the lab. She couldn't think about getting matched when her experiments waited. Testing pH levels was a daily task and Sundays were no exception. She had offered to do the work and it was important for her to be there. She picked up her testing kit and data entry device, and started toward the tanks. The sooner she could finish, the sooner she could work on her own projects.

Sundays were quiet with only another person or two checking in on their own experiments. Most people were happy to give their day to God and relaxation. Monday came all too soon.

She knelt by the edge of the tank and cleared the algae resting on the surface with a special paddle. Using a dropper, she sucked up the green water and squirted it into a test tube, capped it off, labeled the kit, and keyed notes into her data entry device that wirelessly transmitted the information into the main system. When she had her samples, she went to the next tank and repeated the process.

Once there, she knelt down and cleared the algae with her spatula. She heard steps and looked up. It was Mr. Kowalski.

"Why are you here? It's Sunday," he said.

"The tanks need to be tested daily."

"Someone else could do it."

"I volunteered." She didn't know why he disliked her, but it was evident in his glare.

"I thought I told you I didn't want to see you again."

Miss Rhona stood. She was much shorter than Mr. Kowalski and knew her words would have to carry her. "Mr. Kowalski, I don't go out of my way to bother you. Please leave me to do my work."

"You know you're pretty—pretty ugly. No wonder you work everyday. No man will have you. Not with this." He reached toward her with his hands. She stepped to the side, away from the tank. His fingers encircled her neck. She dropped her test kit and tried to fight off his tightening grip around her throat.

"Let go of me!" she choked as she beat on his forearm and kicked his shin.

"Don't you attack me!"

He pushed off and thrust her backside first into the algae tank.

"Aiii!" She clenched her eyes and mouth shut as she hit the yielding surface of the thick algae in the warm water. The weight of her waterlogged clothes made it difficult to surface and she tried not to get her arms and legs tangled in the green mass. She surfaced. Algae hung down her face in a thick clump. She gasped for air and couldn't help breathing in water. She flailed at the surface and coughed out water. He laughed as she wiped algae off her face.

"You horrid man! I'll report you! Go away!"

He reached for a skimming pole, held onto the strainer and extended the pole end out to her. She swam toward it and before she could grab onto the end or react, he hit her on the side of her head and shoulder with the pole. She felt her body go down into the water, submerging her head. As she thrust her arms toward her sides to resurface, the pole hit her squarely on top of her head and sent her downward again. The pain was intense and caused her to exhale. Not knowing her bearings, but feeling somewhat protected by the shield of green, she swam underwater a few strokes before surfacing. Her lungs felt constrained from the lack of air. Taking a chance, she popped up gasping while wiping the algae clear from her face. Upon seeing she was several feet out of the pole's reach, she tread water; the weight of her clothes and shoes dragged her down. It was a losing effort to keep her head above water and away from the thick clumps of algae.

"Enjoy your swim!" He laughed, cast the skimming pole aside, and walked away.

Miss Rhona spit out algae and held her breath as she swam to the opposite side of the tank, hoisted herself up out of the water and collapsed sideways. She breathed in heavily and repeatedly coughed out as Mr. Kowalski walked toward the lab. When he was a safe distance away she balanced on her knees and exploded in tears. Her head, left ear, and shoulder pulsed with sharp pain. She coughed and spit, and tried to hold back the gagging sensation building in her gut. Her head throbbed with ferocity, and she fell to her side, crying and screaming in between gasps, hoping she would not black out before help arrived.

In moments, a man she had seen from time to time appeared along with Mr. Kowalski.

"Look!" Mr. Kowalski said as they ran to her. "She got out! I tried to save her with the skimming pole, but she fought me and went under. I couldn't see her underneath the algae or else I would have gone in myself."

"Thank the Lord you were here," the other man said. "Quick! Let's get her to the clinic."

"Don't touch me! Don't touch me! He tried to kill me!" Miss Rhona stumbled to her feet.

"She's delusional!" Mrs. Kowalski said. "Yuck! She's covered in algae. Poor woman."

Her head spun and she dropped onto her knees. Before she could fall completely over, the two men reached underneath her arms and lifted her up. Miss Rhona tried to fight them off, directing most of her effort toward Mr. Kowalski. She wasn't sure if she could trust the other man, but was more inclined to let him help her. She landed a few glancing blows on Mr. Kowalski and he backed off.

"He did this to me! Get him away from me!"

"I saw her fall and hit her head. If I hadn't come when I did, I'd hate to think what might have happened."

"Come along, Miss," said the man. "Let's get you to the clinic."

He tried to prop her up so she could walk by placing one of her arms over his shoulder, but it was no use. He reached beneath her body and lifted her into his arms. She was aware of the slimy surface of her clothes and how it made carrying her difficult. Her body bounced along as he rushed her toward the main compound, the movement adding to the searing pain in her head. She was vaguely aware of others as she neared the clinic and heard their horrified comments. When the man set her on the ground, she saw Mrs. Porter and knew she was in safe hands. She closed her eyes and relinquished her fate to those present.

In late afternoon Miss Kristian returned to the dorm and cleaned up before the tone sounded for dinner. As she changed in her room, Miss Chastity gave her the news.

"They say she fell into the algae tank and hit her head. She almost drowned. It's just awful. Mrs. Porter is looking after her."

Miss Kristian quizzed her, but Miss Chastity insisted she had no other information.

Mrs. Porter was not present at dinner and the women dined without her. Miss Kristian picked at her food as the women talked about how the accident could have happened. She imagined the scene of Miss Rhona dragging herself out of the tank covered in green slime. No wonder she had no appetite. Her throat felt tight and getting food down wasn't easy.

After dinner, Miss Kristian knocked on the clinic door. No one answered. She tried the handle and let herself in. In a back room of the empty infirmary, Miss Rhona was sound asleep in a metal-framed cot. She went to her and sat on the edge of the bed. Taking her friend's hand in her own, she stroked it and spoke soft words of comfort. After a while she recognized the shuffling gait of Mrs. Porter and stood when her keeper came in the room.

"She's resting easy now," said Mrs. Porter. "No need to worry. She'll come out of this just fine."

A tear escaped down Miss Kristian's cheek and she brushed it aside. "We're all so worried about her."

"Of course you are, and because we all care she's in recovery. Why, if it weren't for Mr. Kowalski, she could have drowned."

"Mr. Kowalski! What does he have to do with this?" Miss Kristian felt a chill run up her spine and down her arms. She rubbed out the gooseflesh.

"He saw her fall and hit her head. He ran for help when she went under."

Miss Kristian tried to remember what had passed between Miss Rhona and Mr. Kowalski. The details escaped her, but her memory of the unpleasant feeling associated with their interaction lingered.

"Her clothes are ruined. I thought to put them in the wash, but I think they're permanently stained. We'll order her a new issue. She'll be up and around in a day or two."

"I see," said Miss Kristian. "I brought her this." She handed Mrs. Porter the apple she had picked the day before."

"Are you sure? It doesn't look very good on the outside."

"But on the inside, it's incredible."

Chapter Ten

On Monday, Mr. Taybert gave Miss Kristian a new assignment, assisting with the van engine tune-up. It was a welcome change from the necessary drudge work she had been given for most of her stay. She reported to the bay and waited until the driver showed up with the van. It was Mr. Stewart.

"You?" she said with a smile. "Mr. Taybert didn't let on."

Mr. Stewart popped the hood and got out of the van. "It was my idea. I thought it would be good to work with Miss Fine Tune, or whatever you call yourself, so we can be together."

Miss Kristian rolled her eyes. She raised the hood and looked over the engine compartment. "I'm your assistant, am I?"

"Not exactly. We're both assisting Mr. Taybert."

She turned toward him. "Say, do you know Mr. Kowalski?"

"I heard he saved Miss Rhona yesterday. I'm sure you're very grateful."

"We'll talk later. Here comes Mr. Taybert."

Miss Kristian listened to Mr. Taybert and under his direction handed him tools and made adjustments. She and Mr. Stewart took turns hooking up the computer and troubleshooting. They discovered an emissions leak was causing poor performance and decided to tackle the problem after the mid-day meal. Upon hearing the tone, they washed up and headed to the lodge.

"Will you do me a favor?" Miss Kristian asked. "See what you can find out about Mr. Kowalski."

Mr. Stewart shrugged. "Sure."

"But don't be obvious. I don't want him to know I'm asking about him."

"Planning a surprise?"

"I'm not sure yet."

At lunch, Miss Rhona's absence was touched upon in conversation. Mrs. Porter was not at the table and no one had news. Miss Kristian ate hurriedly and excused herself to go to the clinic. She arrived at Miss Rhona's bedside to find her awake, sitting up reading. Her long hair was freshly washed and hung loose down the front of her nightgown. Miss Rhona put away her magazine and grinned broadly. The women hugged for a long time.

"I could have lost you," Miss Kristian whispered.

"I'm much better. Mrs. Porter got me up and we took a short walk. I'm not sure where she is now."

"How's your head?"

Miss Rhona winced as she touched the sore parts. "Hurts. Everything hurts."

"Do you remember what happened?"

"They say…"

Miss Kristian placed her fingers over Miss Rhona's lips and felt them quaver. She lowered her hands and saw fear on her friend's face. There was no mistaking it—the brows raised, a grimace as she pulled her mouth down, and the fright in her eyes. Miss Rhona bit her lower lip and held onto Miss Kristian's hands.

"He tried to kill me," she squeaked. "I don't know why! I never did anything to him. No one believes me. They think he's a hero."

"Tell me. I'll believe you."

Miss Rhona recounted her story and when she was through, Miss Kristian brushed aside Miss Rhona's hair to examine her neck. On her left side, the area was bruised where the pole had hit her shoulder. It was reddish-purple and swollen, and a section of her port wine stain looked worse than she remembered. On her right side underneath the whiteness of her jaw was another bruise about the size of a grape.

"This is where he choked you," she said.

Miss Rhona looked over Miss Kristian's shoulder. Miss Kristian turned and saw Mrs. Porter standing in the doorway.

"You've seen this, haven't you?" Miss Kristian said. "This is where his thumb grabbed her throat."

Mrs. Porter's face twitched. She moved toward the women, but said nothing.

"Can't you do something?" Miss Kristian stood up and towered over her keeper. "Or Mr. Porter—he can do something, can't he? He can order him to stay away. Or he could send him away! Please!" She grasped Mrs. Porter's upper arms. "Help us!"

Mrs. Porter took a sharp breath. "I, I can't make any promises."

Miss Kristian hugged her and went back to work.

That evening, heat lightning spread silently across the sky. It was warm out and the women had their windows open with screens in place to keep out the mosquitoes. Miss Kristian felt like going for a walk, but she lay on her bed with the lights off listening to the quiet slumbering noises coming from Miss Chastity. There was something about the repetitive motion of walking that freed her mind to solve problems, which at the moment seemed insurmountable. She touched her foot to the bottom of the top bunk, but there was no one up there to feel it.

She imagined fixing up the buried snowmobile with the

help of Mr. Porter. She had already told him about her find and suggested it would make a good project. Other men would have to work on it, but when it was ready, she and Miss Rhona would use it to escape in the middle of the night. Or, Mr. Porter could help her recreate the needed parts in the mechanics' bay before taking them into the woods where she would slowly, but surely, make a usable vehicle. She would fill the glass bottles from the shed with fuel and hide them in the cabin. When everything was set, she and Miss Rhona would sneak away in the middle of a snowstorm and cross Lake Michigan to Green Bay, Wisconsin. Once in the United States, sympathizers would help them travel through Minnesota to Canada where they would ask for asylum.

Of course it would never work. The ice cutters would keep the bay from freezing. There was no way they could carry enough fuel. The Fleet would catch up to them in no time. The whole thing was ludicrous.

Maybe they wouldn't have to leave the Protectorate. They could build an underground shelter no one could find—an earth cave. She would hunt or fish during the day while Miss Rhona tended to their underground greenhouse. They would catch rainwater, twist ropes out of grapevines and fashion clothing out of hides. They would live a simple life in peace, except the Protectorate would locate them by their chip implants.

Light flashed into the dark room and she imagined being hit above her head by a bolt of lightning, a powerful jolt of electricity capable of transforming her defeatist thoughts into a stroke of brilliance. Stunned, she would suddenly have the answer of how to save Miss Rhona—and herself.

Miss Rhona was allowed to come back to the dorm for more rest, and when she did return to work, it was not testing pH levels. She was confined to the lab. Her supervisor thought it best to keep her in the company of others, rather than risk her health from another unexpected clumsy maneuver, and assigned her to biofuel research and development. It was an unexpected promotion.

Miss Kristian and Mr. Stewart continued their work on the van. After the tune-up, they replaced the brakes and repaired rust spots. Mr. Taybert showed them how to perform a radiator flush on the contained unit.

"Seems odd to winterize now when it's so hot," said Miss Kristian.

"They say we're in for a cold winter," Mr. Stewart replied.

"Oh? Who says that?"

"I heard some people talking. They say this might be the coldest winter we've had in twenty years."

"How can they know that now? It's at least ninety degrees today."

"I don't know. Mr. Taybert must think so because he ordered sub-zero anti-freeze this year for all the vehicles. We'll find out this winter."

Mr. Porter walked into the mechanics' shed and asked about their work. They showed him the progress they'd made on the van.

"Mr. Stewart, I'm going to borrow your work mate."

"If you must," Mr. Stewart winked. "As long as you promise to bring her back."

Miss Kristian removed her protective gloves, squirted cleaner onto her hands and wiped off the mess with a clean rag. She and Mr. Porter walked into the bright sunlight away from the mechanics' shed.

"Wanted to get back to you, Miss Kristian, about your project idea. Show me this buried treasure you've found."

They walked down the road and when they got to the turn-off, Miss Kristian decided to say she had found the cabin one day while exploring on her own. She didn't like having to share her special place with anyone else, not that Mr. Porter would have a clue about what she and Miss Rhona had been doing. She took him through the forest and meadow, figuring it didn't matter who knew about the area, for she and Miss Rhona were never going to be together again, not now or ever. She pointed out the cabin and took him to her find. She showed him the tools she uncovered from the fallen shed and suggested they dig out the snowmobile.

Mr. Porter examined what he could see of the machine.

"This one's not too different than the ones Mrs. Porter and I used to run around on. Hard to tell half-buried."

"Do you think it's worth digging up?"

"Won't know until we try. Hand me a shovel."

While Mr. Porter dug in with a shovel, Miss Kristian broke up the dirt on the opposite side with a usable hoe. As they labored, Mr. Porter muttered about the poor condition of the snowmobile—the rust, bent parts, and so on, yet he continued to dig.

"Here," he said, handing her the shovel. "Get to work on your side while I clean this off."

Miss Kristian dug around the machine, being careful not to damage it. Mr. Porter bent down and used a glove to scrape away dirt caked on the surface. When the two finished, the snowmobile looked like it had been dropped into a hole.

"Well," he said shaking his head, "it's in bad shape. Looks like it was abandoned and left to the elements. And then what? Can't say, but maybe the creek rose and flooded the dang thing." He kicked the dirt with his shoe and cursed under this breath.

"Can we fix it?" she asked.

"Have you told anyone about this?"

"No."

"Well, don't."

Miss Rhona was the only other person who knew about the snowmobile and mentioning her would be foolish. This was the first time Miss Kristian had spent any time with Mr. Porter. He seemed thoughtful, though a bit crusty, and she hesitated to question him further.

"Need to think," he said. "Drop your shovel and let's go. If anyone asks where you've been, you tell them to come see me, and that'll be the end of it."

Zoe Amos

Chapter Eleven

A mid-summer assembly was called. Mr. Browne came down on the community shuttle to see his daughter. She showed him the work they'd done on the farm camp van and he noticed how she beamed when running her hands along the front quarter panel where she and Mr. Stewart had patched a line of rust.

"Will we be seeing Mr. Stewart later?" he asked.

"Yes. Right now he's with his parents. I saw them earlier."

"Where's Miss Rhona?"

"She's busy today. Miss Analise brought in her older brother to meet Miss Rhona. He's a doctor." She noticed her father hesitate and guessing his thoughts added, "For a possible match."

"Excellent!"

Miss Kristian forced a smile. She wanted to tell him about Miss Rhona's so-called accident, but restrained herself, especially since her telling of it would differ from what others believed. It was Miss Rhona's word against Mr. Kowalski's. Presenting her side of the story with no logical reason for Mr. Kowalski's abominable behavior would only create more trouble.

"You said you had something to show me," she said.

They walked to the green area outside the lodge and when another family arose from a picnic table, they took their seats. Mr. Browne fished out a small packet.

"This is for you." He unfolded a piece of thick paper and inside was a photograph. "I thought you might want it."

She turned the photo toward her. "This is mother, isn't it?"

Mr. Browne nodded. "Zarah didn't have your height, but she was strong. We met at the mill. She could carry a fifty-pound bag of feed on her back and toss it onto a skid or into someone's truck. She'd get offended if anyone tried to help. I think you two are much the same. When she had her mind set on something, she went for it—including me. She told me to put in a request for her after I'd known her about six weeks. Your mother was a beautiful person and you take after her."

Miss Kristian lightly touched her mother's cheek on the photograph, knowing some things would never be. "We look alike." She turned it over. "Zarah" was printed on the back in faded letters.

"In this photograph, she's not much older than you are now. She would be proud of you. Twenty years is a long time to miss someone. In case you didn't know, the Stewarts and I finished your legal paperwork. All we have to do is wait until you're of marrying age. You'll cleave to your husband and my work will be done."

"Father, you make it sound so final. I'll be able to visit you. There must be a mill near Sault Saint Marie. You could transfer there and live with us in the Stewart home. There are plenty of extra rooms. Would you like that?"

Mr. Browne smiled. "Nothing is more important to me than your happiness. Let's get you married and settled first. Then we'll see."

They went back to the lodge and when Miss Kristian spotted the Stewarts, her father excused himself to go speak to her keeper about future arrangements. He was gone a long time, but the Stewarts fawned over her and made the time pass. They spoke of all the wonderful things they would do together and how Miss Bettina couldn't wait for her new sister to be in the house, and on and on, until Miss Kristian felt she had already moved in.

Mrs. Stewart handed her a small velvet box. Inside was a pair of diamond stud earrings. "For your wedding day," she said.

Miss Kristian gasped at the sparkling gems. "I don't know what to say. Are you sure? We aren't married yet."

"Yes, I'm sure. You're already like a daughter to me."

"Thank you!"

They hugged and Miss Kristian had a glimmer of what it would feel like to have a mother.

The Stewarts were among the last of the visitors to leave. Miss Analise's brother, Dr. Messer, had returned to the hospital. The sisterhood was chatty at dinner. Everyone shared their day, including Miss Rhona.

"We got on fairly well," Miss Rhona said. "We talked about working in a lab, things many people don't find interesting unless you actually work in one, which he does. He sees patients, too."

"Will you see him again?" asked Miss Betsy.

"He told me he would come again next assembly," Miss Analise said. "I think it looks good."

"That sounds very promising. Miss Rhona, you deserve someone you can talk to about scientific things," said Miss Julie. "I hope you'll be as happy as I am. I'll be getting married in January! Can you believe it?"

"Oh, Miss Julie!"

"That's so exciting!"

"What wonderful news!" said Miss Kristian.

"Congratulations! I can see you're so happy!" said Miss Rhona. "I hope we all can know the kind of love you two share." She looked at Miss Kristian out of the corner of her eye and then smiled brightly at Miss Julie.

"I'll have to show you how to make my meat pasties before you go," said Miss Chastity.

"Would you? He'll like those. They're good."

"Will you show me, too?" Miss Rhona said.

"Good idea. You need to cook up something in the kitchen instead of the lab!"

Everyone laughed, even Miss Kristian who could see what the future had in store for them both.

Chapter Twelve

O ppressive heat made working in the mechanics' bay difficult. All summer, hundred degree afternoons kept the area stifling, even with the bay doors wide open. On such days, Miss Kristian felt rivulets of sweat run down between her breasts. She wore a bandana to keep moisture from running into her eyes, and though she pinned her braid into a bun, by afternoon it unraveled. She hated to pin it up again with greasy fingers. Sometimes, when Mr. Stewart was working nearby, he would come up behind her and give her braid a tug. It was playful and she didn't mind.

"Hot day to be cleaning corn pickers," he said after he sneaked up behind her.

"Today's much better than yesterday. I think we're in for more rain tonight. Hope it cools things down. The seasons are starting to change. You're lucky. I can tell you've been riding in air conditioned comfort."

"Yep!" he laughed. "I can't imagine how they did it in the old days."

"In the old days, the temperature wasn't in the upper seventies in October. Anyway, I think they used to finish harvesting corn in September or sooner."

"The leaves are changing nicely. I love autumn and all the colors."

Mr. Taybert joined them. "If you two lovebirds are done working, then get out of here before I find something else for you to do."

Miss Kristian cleaned up and the two headed out for a walk. They started down the dirt road that divided the cornfields from the forest.

"Remember you asked me about Mr. Kowalski?" Mr. Stewart asked.

"Oh, yes. That was a while ago. It may not matter at this point, but tell me."

"I learned two things about him. He was sent to the farm camp and he's got a temper. He's gotten into fights before. Once he gave his dorm mate a bloody nose."

Miss Kristian shook her head. "Men. You don't see women doing that sort of thing."

"Some men just like to fight. Maybe that's why he was sent here."

They walked in silence and eventually passed the area where she and Miss Rhona used to duck into the forest. Her gaze lingered as she thought of the times they had loved one another in the meadow.

"What are you looking at?" Mr. Stewart asked.

"The trees. I love the aspens. With all the rain we've had this summer, they're such a pretty gold."

He stopped walking. "Like your hair," he said, "such a pretty gold. Pretty eyes. Pretty smile. Pretty you."

He took her in his arms and kissed her. She felt his mouth on hers like an invader. She squirmed and he held her more tightly. She struggled, but he persisted, kissing her mouth and face. Panic set in and she pushed him off.

"Mr. Stewart!"

"I love you, Miss Kristian. I thought by now…"

Her heart pounded. All the friendly times they shared and the planning for her to be Mrs. Stewart felt jagged and unyielding as the reality of the future cut into her chest, making it hard to breathe. She had given her heart to another and her love had never ceased. The thought of making love to a man, even this kindly man who loved her, was repulsive. Feeling his hands on her body, and worse…the duties of being a wife made her shudder. She felt ill and placed her hand over her breast. She was tempted to run away as far as she could go, leaving her world behind. She would run like her life depended on it, holding Miss Rhona's hand because there was no other option that made sense.

"I'm sorry," she said. "Some things take a little more getting used to."

"No, I'm sorry," he said. "I told you I wouldn't kiss you and here I am acting like an animal."

They walked back and engaged in small talk. Miss Kristian couldn't wait to see Miss Rhona, believing the mere sight of her would cleanse Mr. Stewart from her lips. She imagined herself sprinting back to the dorm where she would take Miss Rhona by the hand and run off into the woodsy far reaches of Superior Protectorate. They would cut the chips out of their arms, smash them into the ground, and never stop running until they found isolation. She continued her conversation with Mr. Stewart, yet everything else, her mind, her heart, her emotions, were with Miss Rhona. When she and Mr. Stewart parted, she smiled and squeezed his hand to assure him he was still in her good graces.

After dinner, Miss Kristian whispered to Miss Rhona, "Meet me."

Miss Rhona looked startled, but as the others headed to the dorm, she and Miss Kristian dawdled and then headed down the road.

"What's this about?" asked Miss Rhona.

"I want to show you something."

They looked carefully for others before scurrying into the forest. The path was a little muddy from the last rain, but neither seemed bothered by it, nor the wet greenery that left damp spots on their clothing as they passed. Miss Kristian guided her through the meadow to the other side of the forest. They rounded the corner of the cabin and stopped.

"It's gone!"

Miss Kristian looked at Miss Rhona in shock. At their feet was a large empty hole.

"This is where the snowmobile was? Remember?"

"Yes."

"Someone's dug a ramp and pulled it out." She started crying. "No. No!"

Miss Rhona touched Miss Kristian's arm. "I don't understand. What's this all about? There's never enough snow to use a snowmobile anymore, and that thing was a pile of rusted junk."

"I had this idea," Miss Kristian cried, "that somehow we'd be able to fix it up, and, I don't know, get away!"

"From the farm camp?"

"Yes! From everything! It was a crazy idea. I told Mr. Porter about the snowmobile and brought him out here. We dug it up and he told me not to say anything. That was weeks ago and I haven't been back here since. But look! You can see the tracks where it was pulled out. It was probably him, but where is it? Why hasn't he said anything?"

"How did he get it out of here?"

"I don't know! Maybe there's another road we don't know about." Miss Kristian slumped forward and Miss Rhona hugged her. "I wanted to do it for us," she cried. "You're the one, the only one! I'm meant to be with you, not Mr. Stewart."

While she sobbed, Miss Rhona held her and kissed away the tears that ran down her face. Then they kissed one another and did not stop. They went into the cabin and cleared an area on the grass floor. Quickly, they removed their clothes, hungry for the touch of bare skin. Miss Kristian laid her clothes on the grass beneath them to create a protective layer.

Together again, their love burned as they recreated the joy they had denied themselves. Fingertip to fingertip, breast to breast, they moved together. Miss Kristian breathed in the earthy aromas surrounding them, the crushed grass, the old wood of the cabin and the wonderful fresh, piney smell emanating from the fir trees that dominated the forest. The fragrance of Miss Rhona's skin blended in well and Miss Kristian thought it the nicest of all. Breathing in deeply, the natural outside odors enhanced the feelings surging within her and made her aware of every inch of her own body. It spurred her desire to capture Miss Rhona with sweeps of her fingers, as if her fingertips had a memory of their own that could model her lover like a sculpture at another time when they might be apart.

Miss Kristian felt moisture on her back as she moved over Miss Rhona. The sky darkened, the air cooled and thin drops fell from the sky. Her hands slid across Miss Rhona's skin as she loved her completely. Light flashed above them and she heard the sound of wind rustling in the trees. She licked the drops from Miss Rhona's skin. As the rain increased, she made love and delighted Miss Rhona in a new and wonderful way that excited Miss Kristian, too. Miss Rhona cried out to the forest in pleasure. In turn, Miss Rhona did her best to cover Miss Kristian with her petite body while conveying the passion of her love. Miss Kristian's skin chilled into gooseflesh and her nipples froze into pebble-like points. Inside, she felt waves of warmth roll in reverberating echoes, much like the distant thunder. The rain soaked them and their clothes, but all Miss Kristian wanted was to spend the night making love. They shivered in the falling temperatures and held one another close to maintain their heat.

Lightning lit the sky followed in moments by a low rumble.

"You are my love and my life, and I'll never leave you," said Miss Kristian. "Never!"

"I love you, too. You are my love and my life, and I'll never leave you!"

Rain fell in larger drops as they smothered each other in kisses. They had been gone much longer than they anticipated evidenced by the failing light. The lingering gray sky faded to black and the forest enclosed them in a cloak of darkness. Lightning flashed and in seconds, a loud clap split the air. Wind and wet leaves created a rushing sound in the forest. Debris clattered against the cabin walls and they knew they had stayed too long.

Dressing in wet clothes was not easy. The material stuck to their skin and buttons would not fasten. They did the best they could and put on their shoes. Rain cascaded through the missing roof of the cabin. It seemed to lessen somewhat as they stepped through the pines where boughs sent down large drops that landed on their heads and shoulders. Miss Rhona slipped while traversing the ravine and Miss Kristian helped her up to the other side. They were both covered in mud. As they ran through the meadow lightening shot down, temporarily illuminating their way.

"Where's the opening?" shouted Miss Kristian.

Miss Rhona looked around. "It has to be near here." She pointed. "There? I can't tell."

It was impossible to see with rain sheeting around them. The wind picked up and each minute felt colder than the last.

"Come on, we'll find it!"

Miss Kristian took Miss Rhona's hand and led her into the forest. It wasn't their familiar path and they stepped over logs and around bushes. Miss Rhona's short legs made the going more difficult. Branches clawed at their clothing and tore through material. They untangled themselves as they went along and Miss Kristian helped her around the brush as they cut a new path. They struggled to find clearings that would speed their progress.

They came upon a barbed wire fence. Miss Kristian stepped on the lower wire and tried to lift the upper one as Miss Rhona passed through. Then, she ducked between the wires and caught her back on a barb. Miss Rhona struggled to free her. Lightning crashed overhead and Miss Rhona screamed.

"Are you all right?" Miss Kristian asked as she stood free of the wire. They interlaced their fingers. "I love you!" she screamed into the forest above the noise of the rain. "No matter what happens. Do you hear me? Everybody? I love Miss Rhona!"

Miss Rhona laughed. "I love you!" she yelled.

Miss Kristian held Miss Rhona's face between her hands and kissed her deeply one last time before they made their way out of the forest and jogged down the road.

They rattled the door handle to the dorm and Miss Betsy let them in.

"They're here! Oh, my Lord! What happened to you?"

"Are you all right?" asked Miss Chastity. "Your teeth are rattling together loud enough to wake the devil."

Lightning flashed and the dorm walls vibrated with the low rumble. Mrs. Porter came out of her quarters.

"Quick! Let's get these two undressed and into the shower. Lord, help us. I was just calling for a search party."

The two women were led to the showers. Miss Chastity helped undress Miss Kristian, who watched as Mrs. Porter removed Miss Rhona's dress. The buttons in the back were fastened out of order, a reminder of what they had tried to accomplish in the dark. Miss Kristian was led beneath the shower. Shivering, she crossed her arms tightly and closed her eyes as the warm water cascaded down her body. Miss Chastity scrubbed a washcloth over her backside. The soapy cloth felt rough against her skin. Miss Chastity unbraided her hair and had to reach up to work in shampoo. Small twigs and pine needle bits washed down the drain. The warm water began to have a positive effect and Miss Krisitan slowly relaxed. The shower was turned off and Miss Kristian wiped the water from her eyes. She saw fresh red scratches crisscrossing Miss Rhona's arms and legs, yet was oblivious to her own. Miss Chastity draped a towel over Miss Kristian and led her to the bedroom where she held out a clean cotton nightgown.

Their dorm mates peppered them with questions, but Mrs. Porter waved them off. "Let these two get some rest," she ordered. "Lights out!"

Morning came early to Miss Kristian and Miss Rhona who were told to dress and head to Mr. Harlingen's office before breakfast. The women said little, knowing their fate would change from the consequences of their actions. They sat in a waiting area and nodded at the Porters as they passed through into Mr. Harlingen's office and closed the door. They could hear the murmur of voices as they shifted in their seats. Minutes ticked by and Miss Kristian's stomach growled. The door to the office opened, and Mr. Porter ushered them in.

Mr. Harlingen, with furrowed brow, glared at the women. He tapped a pencil on his desk and pursed his lips. Miss Kristian looked at Mrs. Porter for assurance, but her keeper's expression relayed the obvious. There was nothing she could do to prevent what would happen next. Miss Kristian's heart sank deeper in regret for letting down Mrs. Porter. It hadn't been her intent.

Mr. Harlingen tossed his pencil aside and sipped his tea before speaking. "We had hoped the young ladies who came into our care would serve the Escanaba farm camp honorably. Your former keepers wrote glowing recommendations. In some ways, you two contributed better than expected; however, your inappropriate behavior leaves us no choice." He sighed. "Your time here at the farm camp would have come to an end soon anyway, and I'm personally disgusted. I have to write up a report. It'll be another black mark on our record. First Miss Trudia, and now this. You should be ashamed of yourselves."

Miss Kristian's throat closed and she took a breath to keep from crying. She looked sideways at Miss Rhona who did not look tearful, but defiant.

"Mrs. Porter came to me this morning," he continued. "The evidence against you is circumstantial, and that makes it easier for us and less harsh for you. We've been discussing options for your future. You'll be separated, of course. Miss Rhona," he looked at her, "because you don't have any family of your own, you'll be staying on here. Miss Kristian, you'll be sent to live with your father until your next assignment is determined. Given the situation, Mr. Stewart may decide to rescind his offer to you, but that's his business and the tangle of paperwork is his problem."

Mr. Porter sat squarely in his chair and addressed Miss Kristian. "I'll be taking you up north to your father," he said. "Pack your things."

Miss Kristian swallowed. "Will I have a chance to say good-bye?"

"We asked Mr. Stewart to come. You'll need to talk to him. Mrs. Porter, will you see if Mr. Stewart is here?"

"Come along," Mrs. Porter extended her hand to Miss Rhona. "Let's get you something to eat."

Miss Rhona stood up. Her mouth turned down, yet Miss Kristian couldn't shake the feeling that Miss Rhona had not given up. Mrs. Porter opened the door to the office and led her out. Miss Kristian drank in her last glimpse of Miss Rhona as a tear silently rolled down her face.

"Mr. Stewart," Mrs. Porter said, "Miss Kristian will be out in a moment."

Mr. Harlingen stood, followed by Mr. Porter who showed Miss Kristian the door.

"Go to the dining room when you're done. I'll be waiting for you there," Mr. Porter said.

Miss Kristian looked at Mr. Stewart, while Mr. Harlingen and Mr. Porter exited the waiting area. They closed the door and the two sat alone. Neither spoke. Mr. Stewart cast his eyes downward. He leaned forward and rested his elbows on his knees with his fingers interlaced.

She cleared her throat of tightness. "I'm being sent away. You must be disappointed in me."

He said nothing and the silence prickled her skin.

"I'm sorry," she said. When he did not respond, she touched him lightly and their eyes met. "What did they tell you?"

"Not much. They said you and Miss Rhona spent too much time together and that you had to be separated. They said it was up to me if I still wanted to marry you."

"Do you?"

"I don't know. Do you want me to? I want you to love me. Sometimes love takes time. I don't understand how feelings work. I know you like me, but I think you love her."

Miss Kristian nodded and pressed her lips together.

"No wonder you didn't want to kiss me," he said.

"I do like you and your friendship means a lot to me. I have to leave today. I'm going to live with my father in Marquette."

"I don't have to decide right now. There's no hurry. You're not of marrying age yet."

"You're right. There's no hurry, but you might change your mind. You might meet someone else."

He shook his head. His shoulders slumped forward and he looked at the floor.

"I'm in no position to ask you for anything," she said, "but there is one thing. Will you keep an eye on Miss Rhona? Please? Make sure she's safe and cared for. She met a doctor during the last assembly and they might…"

He lifted his head and renewed hope filled his eyes. "Yes. I'll watch her like a little sister."

She guessed he was thinking if Miss Rhona married her doctor friend maybe they would still have a chance.

"Time," he said. "We'll give it some time."

He smiled weakly at her and she felt her throat constrict.

"You're a good man. What about the jewelry your mother gave me?"

"Keep it for now."

They walked to the dining hall. Everyone had cleared out and they asked the clean-up crew for something to eat. Mr. Porter waited as they downed their breakfast and then stood in readiness. Miss Kristian hugged Mr. Stewart.

"Thank you for understanding."

Mr. Porter walked her back to the dorm where she was handed off to Mrs. Porter.

"Pack your things," Mrs. Porter said. "You might as well take the clothes you've been issued since you've arrived. I doubt we'll be seeing any other women of your size come through. We'll be lucky to get any more women at all."

Miss Kristian felt guilty. The impact of her actions would spread and perhaps deny other girls the opportunity of being assigned to the farm. She felt devoid of strength as she gathered her items onto the lower bunk, folded them, and placed them in her duffle. A wave of light-headedness caused her to sit before she fainted. She spied one of Miss Rhona's camisoles in the laundry bin. On impulse, she packed it with her things and left one of hers tucked into Miss Rhona's bed covers. She brought the bag into the main room.

"Ready?" Mrs. Porter said.

Miss Kristian dropped her bag and burst into tears. "I'm so sorry! I didn't mean to hurt you or anyone else."

Mrs. Porter hugged her charge. Her stout body yielded and Miss Kristian felt the comfort she had not known from her deceased mother. "There, there. It's not as bad as it seems. Young hearts are strong. They heal. Plus you'll be spending precious time with your father. He loves you and he'll have a hand in reestablishing your future. You'll see."

Miss Kristian wiped away her tears. "I'll miss you."

"I'll miss you, too, dear."

"I have to go now, don't I?"

Mrs. Porter led her outside where Mr. Porter waited in the van she and Mr. Stewart had winterized. She searched the immediate area and saw no one. There would be no other good-byes.

As they drove, Miss Kristian looked out the van window through the blur of her tears. A cold front had moved in and her breath fogged the window. She wiped it clear with her sleeve and watched as the farm slipped away behind her. She had nothing to say during the ride and since Mr. Porter was a man of few words they rode in silence.

In little over an hour, they arrived at the mill where her father worked. She waited outside the van and when she saw her father, she ran into his arms and cried. Mr. Porter drove them to her father's home. Mr. Browne put on water to boil while Miss Kristian dropped her bag in her old room. Feeling like a failure, she sat at the table with Mr. Porter and her father, who poured the tea.

"This is the way it is," Mr. Porter said to Mr. Browne. "The Protectorate does not condone friendships like the one Miss Kristian had with Miss Rhona. She's in your care."

Mr. Browne looked stunned. "What? You and Miss Rhona? This makes no sense! What about Mr. Stewart?"

"Mr. Stewart may still want to marry her," Mr. Porter continued. "That's his choice, but I'm going to try my best to make sure that doesn't happen just now."

Tears rolled down Miss Kristian's face.

"Dry your tears, Miss Kristian. I'm on your side."

Miss Kristian froze. "What do you mean?"

"What I mean," Mr. Porter said, "is before this Protectorate nonsense, there was a time when two women like you and Miss Rhona could get married just about anywhere and no one blinked an eyelash. Problem wasn't about folks like you, it was the refugees and the politics associated with the "Water Wars." I lived through the new migration after the East Coast and Florida flooded. At first it was orderly, but then it came on fast. The homeless were in a panic and conflicts escalated. I understand not wanting to live in a tent city, but they took their self-centered, greedy ideas and raped the land without a second thought about those of us who lived here or what might happen when the deer were gone. Squatters started a big fire in the hills, smoked themselves out and ran rough-shod over the local communities. To say things got out of hand was an understatement."

Miss Kristian held her hand over her mouth in shock.

"Furthermore," Mr. Porter continued, "the way things were going, we could have become the next province of Canada. They had enough problems of their own with families sneaking over the border day and night. I don't kid myself. They were minding their own interests—their land and Lake Superior. Conservatives got elected and The Protectorate was formed to create a needed buffer. Otherwise, we would have ended up like the rest of Michigan—struggling in squalor. The Protectorate saved us from that, but we paid a price. Traded freedom for comfort." Mr. Porter grunted. "Remember, Mrs. Porter and I lived here and we didn't want to move. Thought we'd get to stay on our land and live out our lives in relative safety and some sense of normalcy. We're older and we didn't think it would make much difference."

"I had no idea!" Miss Kristian had never heard words like these, so unlike her history lessons of Civil War II.

"It's no accident we're sitting here together," Mr. Porter said. "Do you want to tell her?"

Mr. Browne set down his tea and took her hand. "Listen, when your mother and I fell in love, we didn't know any different. We were young during the war. When the Protectorate was established, we were already here and falling in love, so we got married. But when she had you and became ill, we realized the promises the Protectorate had made were meaningless. Their health care was pathetic. They were going to let her die. I can see you look confused and with good reason. Your mother's nurse was Mrs. Porter and she didn't want her to die either."

"Mrs. Porter! But mother did die. Is that why you're angry?"

"No. We decided to take matters into our own hands by taking advantage of weaknesses in the system. Back then, because the Porters are American Indian, they could travel freely to visit family living on the Menominee reservation in Wisconsin. We took a huge risk. Listen to me. We faked your mother's death."

Miss Kristian gasped.

"The Porters made a false compartment in the back seat of their car and took her to Green Bay where she could get blood transfusions."

"She didn't die?"

"No, she didn't die. After she was well again, Mr. Porter's family was able to get her to Canada."

"Oh, my Lord! I can't believe what I'm hearing? I have a

mother! Then why didn't you go with her? Why didn't we?"

"At first, I only planned to stay behind a short while. I took her from the hospital so presumably she could die at home and made provisions to bury her at sea. Mrs. Porter made a dummy the size of your mother and filled it with tightly packed gravel and dirt. She wrapped it up with batting, and layers and layers of gauze. That's when I met Mr. Porter. We motored five miles out onto Lake Superior and dropped her—the bundle, into the water as the officials watched."

"Oh, father! How horrible that must have been for you! Why didn't you leave afterward?"

"I wanted to, but we couldn't carry out the rest of the plan. They sealed the border to everyone before I could go. Of course I would have taken you with me. For a while it looked like we might be able to bribe a guard at the bridge, but I couldn't pull together the money."

Mr. Porter shook his head. "Tried to help. Didn't happen."

"Is she still in Canada?"

"I believe so," her father said. "Early on, I got a few messages and then they stopped. She told me how to find her and it pained me not to be able to go. I knew she was living a free life and I was happy for her. She made her own decisions of where to live and what to do. She went to university so she could become a teacher. I never fully recovered, but I had to take care of you. I settled in at the mill. I've been saving my money all this time, and the more I save, the more it costs to get across the border. I have no idea how much it costs now. You became my life. It became more important for me to see you to adulthood."

"Now I'm afraid I've ruined everything! I don't know what Mr. Stewart will want to do. I'm sorry you and mother have been apart all these years, but that still doesn't explain what you said before. I'm here because of my friendship with Miss Rhona."

"Yes and no," said Mr. Porter. "You see, I've been planning again with your father. He wanted to make sure you were married and then he was going to try to make a break. It's going to be a cold winter; the likes you've never seen. Thinking the lake will freeze over, something that hasn't happened in decades. We've been working on my old snowmobile because your father thinks he can make it."

Miss Kristian's eyes widened.

"Problem is the thing hasn't run in years."

"I knew it! You took the snowmobile out of the forest!"

"Yes. I took it and I'm raiding it for parts. You didn't know it, but that snowmobile you found could be your father's way out of here. Don't get many chances to work on it—only a couple evenings a week, a day here and there. We needed help, but didn't know anyone we could trust. And when you got yourself in trouble, I knew you were the right person."

Her father sighed. "When I saw you, I figured Mr. Porter stole you away for a couple of days to help out. I'm sorry about you and Miss Rhona. I didn't know. I'm not sure what to think about you two, but I do know I will always love you—the Protectorate be damned!"

Miss Kristian looked at the two men in disbelief. The strange turn of events made her feel shaky and she crossed her arms over her chest. "You want me to help you fix your snowmobile," she acknowledged Mr. Porter and turned to her father, "so you can be with mother?"

Her father nodded. "And you're coming with me."

"Now, hold on!" Mr. Porter interjected. "A second person changes everything, especially one of Miss Kristian's size. Why not smuggle her across the bridge?"

"If she's not marrying Mr. Stewart, she's coming with me," Mr. Browne said.

"It's one thing to risk your life, but hers? That snowmobile isn't a two-seater. What about the extra weight? And extra fuel? I'm trying to help you, not set up a suicide mission!"

Mr. Browne addressed his daughter. "Years ago, I thought that once I made it to Canada by myself, I could get the money to you to cross the bridge. It's far safer. It was an idle dream while you were growing up. I put in a request for you to be sent to the Escanaba farm camp so the Porters could keep on eye on you. I'll still be making decisions for you while you're in this time of transition, but you're an adult now. What do you want?"

Both men looked at her. Rarely had she been asked what she wanted. She bit her lip as she considered sending off her father alone on the chance he would make it to the United States and then Canada. She would be alone with no guarantee of one day being spirited across the Mackinaw Bridge. If she and her father were able to get to Wisconsin or Michigan, they would still be in the unpredictable position of trying to cross the border to Canada. If she stayed put, the Protectorate might stick her with a new assignment to be a nanny in a stranger's home before she could get away. Or, she could pursue Mr. Stewart on the hopes he hadn't changed his mind. Then they would establish their lives in Superior Protectorate. Not only would she never see her father again, she would never have the opportunity to meet her mother or develop the long sought relationship she had missed her whole life. Unfortunately, being with Miss Rhona was not one of her choices and as much as she hoped they might flee together, the best choice at this time was clear.

"Father, I'll go with you," she said.

Chapter Thirteen

Miss Kristian was relieved to hear her first assignment would be working part-time at the feed mill office, arranged at her father's request. As before, she and her father rode the community shuttle into town. She reacquainted herself with the office staff including Mr. Findlay, who had married a woman from town. Her tasks were light and she wondered when her real work would start.

A week later Mr. Porter drove into town. Miss Kristian felt excitement as she donned her overalls. She thought of Miss Rhona every day and missed her greatly. However, anticipating work on the snowmobile and taking an active role in her future helped lift her gloom.

"Your spirits seem better today," Mr. Porter remarked. "True mechanics can't wait to get back to work. Must be your calling."

He drove them to his modest home situated several miles out of town. Surrounding the property were thick stands of pine, their boughs catching the snow flurries before they touched ground. Miss Kristian followed the men to a workshop in a detached garage. Inside, parts were scattered everywhere along with the skeleton of a snowmobile.

"Is this the one you pulled out of the forest?"

"No. This is my old one. Look over there." He pointed toward the back corner at a tangle of parts and twisted metal. "Our challenge is going to be the fuel intake. This old machine of mine's a two-stroke. We need to convert it to ethanol or a biofuel-ethanol mix. This seat here is for one person." He pointed at an item resting on the garage floor. "Rat's nest is what it is. There's a job for you. Strip off that outer layer of material and we'll figure out how to add a second seat to the frame. What do you think, Mr. Browne? Should we go for height or length?"

Miss Kristian picked up a hint of annoyance in his voice, a reminder of the change in plans.

"Where's the diagram? My daughter needs to see what it looked like before we got to this point. I'd like her input."

"It's on the counter."

Mr. Browne retrieved the papers and showed his daughter a schematic illustrating how the parts would fit back together. Modifications would be needed in the form of a bigger fuel tank, or room for storage tanks, plus the conversion from one seat to two.

"If we raise the rear seat," she said, "we'll have room underneath for an extra fuel tank."

"And if you sit up high, you're in for a bad ride. The cold and wind will be merciless."

"Could we raise the height of the windshield?"

"Yes, but then you've got more wind resistance up front and reduced miles per gallon. Everything's a trade-off."

"I'll think on it."

She took a utility knife from the tool chest and sliced into the seat, noting how the material was stitched together. None of it was salvageable. Rats had clawed several holes through the seat and built a warm nest inside. It was empty of vermin. Donning a pair of gloves, she went after the rotted padding. It was sprinkled with feces and came out in hard yellow clumps that partially disintegrated in her touch. She deposited this in the trash and used a wire brush to remove the stuck-on insulation from the frame.

She saw a helmet hanging on the wall and interrupted the men, who were busy trying to free up a frozen part. "Is there another helmet?" she asked.

Mr. Browne looked up. "What are the chances?" he asked Mr. Porter. "I forgot about that."

"That's because you weren't thinking when you decided to toss your daughter onto the back like a sack of potatoes. There won't be one at that old cider mill. Lord knows."

And Lord knows what I've gotten myself into, thought Miss Kristian.

Little progress had been made when Mr. Porter grunted a comment about getting back to the farm camp. He came again the following Saturday and the three of them set to work. On Sunday, the Brownes went to church and returned home with their allotments. Miss Kristian took food with her when Mr. Porter came to fetch them. She cooked up a pot of chili and froze it in portions so her time could be spent in the workshop and not in the kitchen.

They decided to weld a raised second seat onto the frame to allow more room for an expanded fuel tank. Mr. Porter designed a hinged seat, one that would flip up to reveal the fuel cap. Raising the center of gravity, even by a few inches, created a greater possibility of tipping, especially on turns.

"Let's move the skis farther out to the sides. It will add stability," Miss Kristian said.

"Did you have to grow so tall?" Mr. Porter said with a wink.

"While we're at it, we may as well widen the tank. We'll need every drop of fuel," Mr. Browne said. "Any idea what kind of performance we'll get with biofuel?"

"Can't say. In any case, we'll have to strap a container on the back."

"Will there be room to pack clothes?" asked Miss Kristian.

"Wear all the clothes you can. How are you with a needle and thread?"

She gave a thumbs-up sign to Mr. Porter.

"Good, because you're going to need two snowmobile suits. I'll see what I can salvage and bring it 'round to your father's house. You can be sewing when you're not here."

During the following week, Miss Kristian wished she had the material for her sewing project. Rain came down in icy streaks, pelting her windows and downing old leaves to the ground. At every moment, she expected the moisture in the air to snap and turn to snow. Autumn was typically beautiful with crisp days and chilly nights. This year, she felt cheated. Summer had leaped into early winter with its tell-tale sign of hoar frost covering the ground until mid-morning. Thin, gray light peeked through the clouds, never appearing long enough to warm the air or the stiffness that penetrated her limbs.

She thought of Miss Rhona and imagined them together in her lower bunk in the days before Miss Chastity arrived—before all that had happened to keep them apart. She could visualize herself floating southward through the air over the leafless trees to Escanaba, alighting in her old dorm room bed. She could touch the bottom of her foot to the underside of the upper bunk and Miss Rhona would drop her hand over the side, or better yet, would join her inside the sheets where they could curl together in sleep. It was then she remembered the photo of her mother. She had tucked it inside one of the lower slats of the upper bunk where she could see it before lights out. During her hasty departure, she had not thought to take it with her. At least there was a shred of hope she would actually meet her mother one day and hold her in person. Miss Rhona was gone forever.

On more than one occasion, she had thought about writing

a note to Miss Rhona, but hesitated, knowing its discovery would only lead to trouble. She was delighted when the following week, Mr. Porter delivered a letter to her. The plain, lined paper note with its handwritten message was folded small.

"My wife gave this to me," Mr. Porter said.

Miss Kristian took the note and walked off a few steps before unfolding it.

Dear Miss Kristian,

Everyone in the sisterhood misses you and sends their regards, Mrs. Porter included. In fact, it was her idea to send you a note, and for that I am grateful. I hope you are well. I am fine.

I am busy working in the lab on my own projects as no others have been assigned. It's an odd feeling not being told what to do, a mix of rejection and relief. I am developing specialized strains of biofuel in an effort to increase potency. Algae works better than corn, but I can only make small batches. Mrs. Porter suggested I let her husband try it in the farm camp van. If you see him at church, ask him about it.

Miss Julie is getting married soon and we are all busy planning for the happy day. Miss Chastity had her meat pasty demonstration. They were delicious and I hope to write down the recipe for you another time.

I have not heard from Dr. Messer, Miss Analise's brother. Mr. Stewart has stopped by to say hello and talk. I am sure you asked him to do this, and again, I am grateful. Mr. Kowalski has been watching me, too. I saw him replace a few PlastiCorn panels over the algae ponds, as many of them have holes, and I've seen him check on me when he thinks I'm not looking. One never knows when an act of kindness may strike.

It snowed here as I'm sure it did in Marquette. We will have the coldest winter I've ever witnessed, and I trust you are warm and cared for by your father. My greatest treasure is an old photograph I found. You look like her.

Warmest regards to you both,

Miss Rhona

"You read this, didn't you?" Miss Kristian asked Mr. Porter.

"Of course."

"Can you get a message back to her?"

"If you have something to say, I'll tell her in person, or Mrs. Porter will."

Miss Kristian thought a moment. "No. Tell Mr. Stewart... tell him to keep an eye on Mr. Kowalski. Something's terribly wrong."

Mr. Browne looked up from his work. "Let me see that." Miss Kristian handed him the letter and he read it. "She sounds all right to me."

"No, father, she's afraid and I'm afraid for her. Mr. Kowalski can't be trusted; that's what she's saying. He hurt her last summer. I think she has reason to believe he may try to hurt her again."

Mr. Porter grunted. "Oh, I heard that story."

"Well, I didn't," said Mr. Browne. "What's this all about?"

Miss Kristian told him what happened the day she "fell" into the algae tanks and how Mr. Kowalski "saved" her.

"I'll keep an eye on Mr. Kowalski and I'll tell Mr. Stewart to get a little closer to Miss Rhona."

"Yes, please do. And tell her I miss her. Tell her I'm fine."

"Now, let's get back to work. Time's wasting. These shock absorbers are practically useless, and with two heavy riders, the weight ratio is already off balance."

Wet snow fell the day before Thanksgiving, and Miss Kristian and her father celebrated in the church basement along with their neighbors. They sent prayers to those less fortunate than themselves, and silently prayed for help with their project and its outcome. They sent prayers out to all whom they loved including Miss Rhona, and for the first time Miss Kristian said a prayer for her mother.

Snow fell again before the previous accumulation disappeared. Large trucks with blades attached to the front were employed on the main streets, and the salt spreaders were out night and day. The storm passed, the sun came out, yet the air did not warm. Snow lingered and rather quickly turned an off color, a light brown that neither Miss Kristian nor her father could ever remember seeing.

Mr. Porter was able to secure material for Miss Kristian, and she worked on the snowsuit sewing project on days when she wasn't at the feed mill or working on the snowmobile, which was starting to take shape.

"I spoke to your ladyfriend," Mr. Porter said one day. "She was able to provide us with micro filters from the lab. The ash that's in the air is playing havoc with our engines. Keeps clogging the air cleaner in the van. Here." He handed a box stacked with micro filters to Miss Kristian. "See what you can do with this. You can't be cleaning out the air filters in the middle of the lake, and you can't be messing with the fuel filter either. If the engine dies, so do you."

"Take it easy!" Mr. Browne said. "No one's dying! Don't go scaring my daughter. We're going to make it across the lake or we're not going. Simple as that." He nodded his assurance toward his daughter.

Miss Kristian decided to make an air filter for Mr. Porter's van using the micro filter. It was a test. If it worked there, she would then apply the same knowledge to the snowmobile. She unscrewed the air filter from the van and rinsed it clean. Dirty water ran down the drain of the utility sink.

Ash was everywhere, but it was anyone's guess as to its source. News from the outside didn't exist and the Protectorate had merely acknowledged the problem with little fanfare. She decided to make masks out of the micro filters for the three of them. Breathing the fine dust could be harmful. When she looked up in the sky, it was hard to tell ash from cloud, for even when snow seemed to clear the air of particles, the ash continued to rain down in a mist so fine, she was never sure that was what she saw. It accumulated against curbs on the street, and the wind blew it around in slithering streaks like brown, dry snow. Some days it seemed to disappear into the forest, only to return again. Fine grit appeared on their work surfaces and Miss Kristian was not surprised when Mr. Porter installed PlastiCorn sheeting to cover the garage door and workshop window.

She loved the fresh snow and there was plenty to love. Mr. Porter was unable to come up for Christmas due to hazardous driving conditions. Plows pushed the snow into ever growing piles, making it difficult to see around the huge dingy brown mounds outlining byways. She and her father took the community shuttle to church for midnight services and almost didn't make it back. When the driver dropped them off at their door, the wind pushed at them in angry blasts. Miss Kristian slipped, but her father caught her. He managed to keep his footing and get her inside.

Snow fell all night and in the morning when Miss Kristian woke, she gazed out onto a thick blanket of white. Over a foot of fresh snow covered everything in unrecognizable white hills. The sun made the snow glitter in prismatic sparkles that were so bright, she had to shield her eyes. An unusual quiet filled her ears. There was no road noise. She heard the wind blow and the faint sound of a shrub scratching against her window.

"I've never seen anything like it!" she exclaimed to her father while pouring his tea at breakfast.

"I remember blizzards like this when I was a child. We took a snow day and didn't go to school. Your mother and I made a giant snow castle once. We cut out blocks and pieced them together. It was the size of a playhouse and we stayed there all day even though our teeth were chattering."

"I don't know that I want to go outside. It's freezing out there."

"We need to dig out," he said, casting his eyes toward the front windows. His face softened and he looked dreamy. "This is why we're going to make it. I can imagine the ice buildup on the lake. Today is Christmas and the people of Superior Protectorate are honoring the day in quiet contemplation. The land is still. Just imagine the lake frozen over from one end to the other as if we were leaving today. You and I will breeze along, steady and sure. You'll hold on tight as we cross over hidden bumps in the ice where waves have pushed up and frozen solid. I can almost see your mother waiting for us on the shore, waving her arms, guiding us in. She'll know who you are at first sight. For her, it will be like looking in the mirror."

Miss Kristian could imagine the scene. She knew her mother wouldn't be waiting for them on the Wisconsin shoreline, but nonetheless, the mental picture made her smile.

"When are we going to plan our route?"

"Soon. I've already discussed it with Mr. Porter. It occurs to me that the islands could be hard to make out covered in white. We'll travel at night and arrive at daybreak. We'll need two sets of goggles, yellow for night or gray skies, and dark, protective sunglasses so we don't get snow blindness."

"Will we be able to see the lights on the bay?"

"Not until we get close. Thunder Bay is a long way off and by then there should be daylight."

"You mean Green Bay."

"No, Thunder Bay."

"In Canada? What are you talking about? I thought we were heading to Wisconsin, to Green Bay. Or if we had to, go across Lake Michigan to Charlevoix," she said.

Mr. Browne shook off his reverie. "No, dear. We're crossing Lake Superior. That's what this is all about."

"Lake Superior?" Miss Kristian sat upright. "That's crazy! It's huge! We can't do that!"

Mr. Browne reached forward to take his daughter's hand, but she pulled away. "Yes, it's a huge undertaking, but we can do it! You thought we were going to cross from Escanaba?" She nodded. "There's no assurance it will freeze over to the south. Anyway, the ice cutters will free up Green Bay and Lake Michigan to keep the freighters moving beneath the Mackinaw Bridge. The cutters haven't crossed Lake Superior in years. The locks are already shut down and that part of the border is heavily guarded. Sure, it's a mere stones throw to Canada from the Soo, but we wouldn't last a minute crossing there. You think others haven't tried? And that's assuming we can get the snowmobile there without being stopped. These things aren't legal, you know."

"Every time you talked about 'the lake,' I, I thought...," her mouth felt dry and her words trailed. "How do we know Lake Superior will freeze over?"

Mr. Browne sat back in his chair. "We don't, not for sure, but it's much colder. Look at it out there. This is only the beginning. By the end of January, the ice should be thick from end to end. We've already had record cold. The temperature hasn't been above freezing for days, weeks!"

"No wonder Mr. Porter called this a suicide mission! Why are you doing this?"

"Because twenty years is long enough. Do you know what it's like to be apart from the person you love for twenty long years?

This may be my only chance. Our only chance! Just think—we'll be reunited and you'll finally get to know your mother. You'll be able to make up for all those years you missed."

Miss Kristian fisted her hand and bit her knuckle. She thought about Miss Rhona. They had only been apart a couple of months and at times it was unbearable. At night, she gathered the blankets around her and cried so her father wouldn't hear. Her heartache was devastating, the pain in her chest, real. Anguish spread through her entire body, stiffening her into a quasi-state of paralysis that could only be cured by Miss Rhona's touch. Sleep would come. She had her work and could get through the day, only to feel the emptiness repeat itself at night. She had hoped with time her feelings would dissipate. They had become stronger. What had it been like for him? Was the thought of never seeing his wife again worth a shot at trading his life?

"Lake Superior," she said. "I don't know. I don't know!" She went into her room and closed the door. She took out the small camisole she had taken from Miss Rhona's things and held it to her face as a source of comfort.

She heard her father knock around the kitchen. As tableware clattered against the counter, she pictured him making breakfast, eating alone—his established routine on the days she had not lived with him. She loved her father. He was a fine man, and she understood the love shared between father and daughter was not the same as feelings shared with a special someone. Of course he wanted to be with his wife. And once they crossed the lake, would she then spend the rest of her life pining for Miss Rhona? Or perhaps it didn't matter for her. She would never be with Miss Rhona whether she stayed in Superior Protectorate or traveled miles away to Canada. The result would be the same. She heard the front door close. Her father had gone out to shovel and she got dressed to help, donning the snowsuit she had made for the trip.

Mr. Porter arrived on January second.

"No point in coming until they plowed," he said. "My neighbor down the way has a snow blower and was kind enough to clear my driveway. There's a nice Christmas present. Speaking of which…" He pulled out a small package. "For you." He handed a wrapped item to Miss Kristian.

"Thank you!"

It was a jar of cherry jam with a pretty calico cloth circle glued to the lid.

"Look, father. How lovely! Did Mrs. Porter make this?"

"It's from your friend."

Miss Kristian tried not to blush.

"Look at this here." Mr. Porter pulled a helmet out of his sack. "Don't ask how I got it."

"Hey!" Mr. Browne said. "A helmet for you. Try it on."

It was in good condition. Miss Kristian noted there were few scratches in the curved protective shield that snapped onto a visor. The helmet felt small going on. She stopped midway and removed it.

"I'm afraid it's too small."

The three looked at each other.

"Try again," her father said. "Try putting it all the way on and maybe it'll be roomier."

She forced it on. The padding did nothing to relieve the vice-like pressure. Her nose pressed against the shield and she removed it quickly.

"Ow!" She rubbed out the sore spots. "This must be for a child. I need an adult-size like yours. I appreciate you trying."

Mr. Porter took the helmet. He found a stray nail sticking out of the wall and hung it up by the strap. "Well, let's get on with it. We're putting the new fuel tank in place."

Miss Kristian shook her head in disappointment. Mr. Porter had gone to some trouble and now would have to find another helmet. "How's Mrs. Porter?" she asked.

"She's fine, not that she would complain. Sends her regards."

"Do you have any other news from the farm camp?"

"One other thing. Mr. Stewart and Mr. Kowalski got into a fist fight. My wife treated them both. Mr. Stewart had a cut on his lip and Mr. Kowalski sported a shiner."

"Oh, no! What was that about?"

"I believe they were fighting over Miss Rhona."

"What?" Miss Kristian felt her heart pound. "That's impossible! I don't know why, but Mr. Kowalski does not like Miss Rhona."

"And Mr. Stewart does?" asked Mr. Browne. "You told him to spend more time with her."

Miss Kristian slapped her forehead and caught her fingers in her hair. "No! Something's very wrong!"

"Maybe you're wrong. I think Mr. Kowalski likes Miss Rhona. He finds reasons to see her and he doesn't want Mr. Stewart butting in."

"No! There's something wrong about Mr. Kowalski. I don't trust him. He needs to stay away from her." Tears burst from her eyes. "She can't stay there, it's dangerous. He's dangerous."

Mr. Browne put his arm around his daughter. "It was probably a misunderstanding. Young men are quick to throw a punch or two and then the fight's over."

"What happened to Dr. Messer? Why hasn't he requested her?"

"I don't know about that," Mr. Porter said, "and I don't know much about Mr. Kowalski. I'm not his keeper."

"I feel so helpless!" she gripped her father's jacket and shook him in frustration, landing her forehead against his chest.

"Calm down, Miss Kristian. I'm sure it's nothing," said Mr. Porter.

"You don't understand. I have to get her out of the farm camp before Mr. Kowalski does something terrible again. No one cares about Miss Rhona except me. I'm sorry, father, I know you care about her, too, but not like I do. I...I...I love her! I'm in love with her! There, I said it. That's why we've been separated. I don't want Mr. Stewart any more than she wants to be with Dr. Messer. We're meant to be together," she sobbed. "I have to see her. I have to be with her. My life is meaningless without her!"

Mr. Browne walked his daughter to a chair and sat her down. She held him around the waist and cried into his body. It was chilly inside the workshop, even with the space heater on, and he rubbed her back over her layered clothing. Mr. Porter tossed over a clean shop rag and Mr. Browne offered it to his daughter. She blew her nose and cried a little more.

"Miss Kristian, you should make yourself some tea, eh? Go in the house and warm yourself."

Miss Kristian went into Mr. Porter's kitchen and removed a package of deer stew from the freezer. She let it slowly warm on the stove as she thought about the myriad events and feelings she had been through in such a short time. She recalled her dreams of escaping with Miss Rhona. The idea was never realistic. Even if they could have stolen a running snowmobile, they would have been caught before they left Escanaba or drowned in Lake Michigan. She wasn't sure which was worse. Now the dreams of escape had been revived by men who could make it happen. Their combined effort would get the snowmobile running, and after a twenty-year wait, she would never deny her father the opportunity he had long sought.

She imagined what it might be like to see her mother, an

older version of herself according to her father. What would it feel like to hug her? Would her mother stand by her side in the kitchen while giving instructions on how to make the best meat pasty in town? Was her mother still as much fun as her father remembered from the times of their youth? There was only one way to find out, and there was always hope that once there, they would find a way to smuggle Miss Rhona into the country to be with them. A twenty-year wait seemed intolerable, but she couldn't imagine not trying. Her father had persevered. Perhaps she was more like him in that way.

After she had eaten, she packaged up a sealed container of hot stew with bowls and spoons, and walked out to the workshop. She ladled it out. The men stopped their task and warmed their hands against the bowls. They had bolted the fuel tank in place and connected the fuel line. On a nearby counter, she spotted the fuel cap fitted with a new gasket Mr. Porter had cut from a piece of rubber. The old one had disintegrated.

"What's next?" she asked. "Can we start it up?"

"Well," Mr. Porter said, "as much as I'd like, that's not going to happen here. Too much noise. We've managed to get this far without alerting the neighbors. I'm thinking Hiawatha National Forest."

"There are too many cabins there," Mr. Browne countered, "and we need a flatter surface for a test run—like an open lake."

"I know a closed logging road southeast of Gwinn. The snow tires on the van won't be enough. I've got some chains lying around here somewhere. Hope they fit. We can't get stuck out there. Lord knows what we'd say."

Miss Kristian wasn't too keen on the plan, but no one asked her opinion. They had wheels to put beneath the snowmobile and a ramp. With the three of them pushing, they could load the snowmobile into the back of the van. But what about when the test was over and it had to go back in the van? Could they do it on a snowy road? She collected the dirty bowls, and after returning them to the kitchen she decided to take a walk.

Mr. Porter's house was in a semi-rural forested area and though the neighbors' houses were hidden from view, they weren't too far away. She tromped through the snow to the house next door. No one was home and she retraced her steps. There were only trees behind Mr. Porter's house. As she approached the house on the other side, she hid behind a clump of birch and saw a man and a woman board the community shuttle before it drove away. She ran back to the workshop. The cold air hurt her lungs as she panted.

She let herself in. "While you two have been planning how to take the hard road," she said trying to catch her breath, "I checked on your neighbors." She reported what she saw.

"No time to lose, eh? I brought special biofuel with me, courtesy of your Miss Rhona. She thinks it's for the van."

Mr. Porter retrieved a two gallon red container and lugged it into the workshop. He poured a small amount into the snowmobile's tank and twisted the cap shut.

"Here goes."

He turned the key and pressed the starter. A weak noise emanated from the converted engine. He let go and tried again with the same result.

"Oh, no! The battery didn't hold the charge," Miss Kristian said.

Mr. Porter turned on the front headlight. It glowed a dim yellow and he tried the starter. It turned over once with great effort.

"We can't run this with the doors closed anyway," Mr. Porter grumbled.

"No, not the garage door. Open up the regular door, then, and let's get the charger hooked up."

Mr. Porter plugged in the battery charger and clamped it to the snowmobile. He was about to give it another try when he paused. He bowed his head and Miss Kristian could see his lips move as he uttered a silent prayer. He took a breath and exhaled loudly. He repeated the steps. Key in. Turn. Press the starter. It turned slowly, paused, and turned again. It sounded horrible, but the sounds it made were encouraging. The engine made an uneven rhythmic noise as if warming to its task, and it caught. Mr. Porter released the starter button and the engine died. He tried it again. The engine turned more quickly this time. It caught, made a dry cough, and died again.

"Do you think it's getting enough air with the micro filters?" Miss Kristian asked. "It's one thing on the van where you've got a much larger intake."

"She's right," Mr. Porter said. "Find a pin. Punch a few tiny holes in this filter and see if that helps. It wouldn't hurt to prime the pump either. There's no fuel in here whatsoever."

"We've no business taking this anywhere until we work out the problems here," said Mr. Browne. "Keep an eye on the road," he told his daughter. "Hurry back when we need to stop." He turned to Mr. Porter. "You want to put a few drops of fuel inside or just give it another go?"

Miss Kristian started down the long driveway. Another community shuttle drove by and she was glad the driver didn't stop. She could see down the road. The van drove past the neighbor's house. The road was fairly clear and she noticed the snow wasn't as dark as it had been before the blizzard.

There was little to see by the side of the road and her thoughts turned to Miss Rhona. She imagined standing next to her friend, who made notes while looking into the microscope or distilling small batches of biofuel. Miss Rhona was involved in her own world. In the evenings, she imagined the sisterhood would provide moments of entertainment. Would Mrs. Porter tell Miss

Rhona about the escape after they left? She jumped from thought to thought. There would always be unanswered questions and she would have to live with them when she and her father were safe in Canada.

Cold air pinched her cheeks and she shifted her weight to stay warm. Her nose ran and she sniffed to keep the moisture from freezing on her upper lip. A thermometer on the outside of Mr. Porter's garage read four degrees. It would dip well below zero again in the night. After fifteen minutes, she wondered how she would cope on the back of a snowmobile with the wind chill effect when she was freezing on a day with no breeze. A cardinal sang in the distance. She heard a roar coming from the workshop, and the cardinal was silenced. She grinned. The engine stopped. It started. It sputtered unreassuringly and kept going. This pattern went on for another fifteen minutes with breaks of silence when the men must have been making adjustments. She tried to huff away the cold air without breathing through her mouth. She marched in place and held her arms close to her chest. Small ice crystals touched her chin where her breath froze onto her scarf.

After another moment of silence the engine started again. This time, it ran fairly well. She could hear it rev up and calm down, rev up, calm down. It was quieter at idle and running smoother than before. She imagined her father and Mr. Porter celebrating inside. It died again and started right up. She saw a community shuttle slow as it reached the neighbor's house and she ran to the workshop.

Chapter Fourteen

Since the last blizzard, Miss Kristian could tell the air had cleared by looking at the snow. It glistened in the sunlight with beautiful sparks of yellow, blue, purple, and orange, much like the diamond earrings Mrs. Stewart had given her. It would not be proper for her to keep them and she wasn't sure how to explain to Mr. Stewart that she wouldn't be marrying him. A face-to-face conversation would be hard. Returning the jewelry was the least she could do.

"Father," she said as they relaxed at his home, "I have something that belongs to Mr. Stewart."

"Give it to Mr. Porter. He'll return it."

She thought about this, left the room and returned with the small velvet box. She opened the hinged top and revealed its contents. "Look," she said. "Mrs. Stewart gave me these thinking I would be a part of their family."

Mr. Browne raised his eyebrows. "Are they real?"

"I suppose."

"They're worth a lot, then. Something like this could be used to get you across the border. Did you ever think of that?"

"No. I don't know about these things."

Mr. Browne held out his hand and she dropped the earrings into his palm. "I don't know much about these things either, but I know they're worth a lot of money. Someone would pay for these, or you could use them as a bribe."

"It doesn't seem right for me to keep them. I need to tell Mr. Stewart I can't marry him, or I'll be gone."

Mr. Browne examined the diamonds in the light. Colorful sparkles scattered as he turned the gems in his fingers. "You want to talk to Mr. Stewart in person, eh? Have you thought about what to say? He'll ask you why you'd prefer to marry someone the Protectorate assigns to you than him. It's a legitimate question and you'd better have an answer."

"What do you think I should do?" she asked.

"I think Mr. Stewart is an honorable man who deserves to be treated fairly." He handed her back the earrings. "These could buy freedom for Miss Rhona. Think about that."

While standing in line for her allotments after church, Miss Kristian saw her father speak with Mr. Porter. Unfortunately, Mr. Porter had not been able to get away during the week and she hoped he would not have to hurry back to the farm camp. She and her father took the community shuttle back to their home and in a short while, Mr. Porter came to pick them up.

"I have a surprise for you," Mr. Porter said to Miss Kristian as he drove up the snow rutted drive to his home.

Miss Kristian's heart began to pound. Was it Miss Rhona? She ran into his house and heard noise coming from the kitchen. Mrs. Porter sat at the table peeling a cored apple.

"Mrs. Porter!" Miss Kristian could barely contain her excitement. Mrs. Porter set down her paring knife. Miss Kristian bent down and the two hugged. "How nice to see you!" she beamed. "How are you?"

"Good. A little creaky. Couldn't make it to church."

"Where is she?"

"Who's that, dear?"

Miss Kristian smile faded. The surprise was sitting at the table and there was no one else. It was almost too much to bear and she turned around to look out the window.

"It's wonderful to see you, Mrs. Porter." She tried to conceal her measured breaths, but it was no use. "I thought maybe... she..." Miss Kristian burst into tears. "How am I ever going to live without her?" she cried.

Mrs. Porter struggled to her feet and put her arm around Miss Kristian. "Tsk! Such heartache! You must put it behind you."

Miss Kristian took a seat as tears rolled down her cheeks and Mrs. Porter offered the dish towel tucked inside her apron.

Mr. Browne came in. "Oh, sorry to interrupt. I came in for tea. Are you figuring out what to do about Mr. Stewart?"

Mrs. Porter shook her head. "What about Mr. Stewart?"

Miss Kristian dried her eyes and explained her dilemma. "I have to tell him it's over and I have to give him back the earrings. Or do you think we should use them to get Miss Rhona to Canada?"

Mrs. Porter looked at Mr. Browne for an answer. He shrugged and looked pained.

"I know there's no easy answer," Miss Kristian said. She picked up the corer and punched it through an apple. When she removed the core, she looked through the red orb. Its heart was gone and she tossed the fruit into a bowl with the others.

The men decided to test run the snowmobile on the old logging road. They were able to load it into the back of the van using a skid fitted with wheels. Miss Kristian visited with Mrs. Porter as snow fell and the smell of apple cobbler filled the house. The afternoon wore on. They served themselves large spoonfuls of cobbler and then prepared dinner. Mrs. Porter talked about

Miss Julie's delightful wedding in the lodge. It seemed to Miss Kristian they talked about everything except what was truly on their minds. It was dark when the men returned. They took their boots off in the mud room and washed up.

"Not the best performance," said Mr. Porter as he sat at the table. "Felt like pulling a mule." He said grace so they could eat.

"I can't imagine it's going to be better with everything else loaded on," said Mr. Browne. "We're going to have to cut weight."

"From where? We got it up to twenty miles an hour. If it'll hold steady, you're looking at a five-hour trip—minimum," he said. "You don't know how rough it'll be until you get out there. And the wind! May the Lord protect you."

"We can't assume it's a straight shot out," said Mr. Browne. "We'll have to slow for variations in the ice and we may have to take wide detours."

"Why?" asked Miss Kristian.

"Remember the ice we saw that time?" Mr. Porter asked his wife without waiting for an answer. "Giant! Waves that froze in mid-air, if that's possible."

Mrs. Porter nodded and hummed. "Yes, that was quite a sight."

"You might find open water. If that happens, head north to Isle Royale."

Miss Kristian imagined traveling miles out of their way to find solid ice.

"We stalled out there," Mr. Browne said. "A couple of times."

Mr. Porter grunted in agreement and Miss Kristian knew he was reminding himself their plan wasn't a sure thing. He would have to let them go, never knowing if they made it or not.

A couple of days later, Miss Kristian was surprised by Mr. Porter when he walked into the feed mill with Mr. Stewart. It was the end of the work day, and he drove them with her father back to the Browne's house. Miss Kristian was happy to see Mr. Stewart, and also conflicted about what to tell him. She had worked out one or two speeches in her head, though the one-sided conversation never played out with realism.

The sun had set, but Mr. Porter and Mr. Browne found an excuse to go outside. She started making dinner. Mr. Stewart stopped her.

"I'm here for a reason," he said. He gestured for her to move with him into the living room. "You've made a decision."

"Maybe you have, too," she said.

"You don't have to tell me. You haven't sent any messages or letters. You could have."

Miss Kristian nodded. "I appreciated you looking in on Miss Rhona for me. I got those messages."

"It doesn't have to end. I still love you. We could marry and I could ask that Miss Rhona be sent to our house."

"She won't do it. I mean, not that she has a choice. She wouldn't be able to cope with me being with you, and I wouldn't be able to either. I couldn't be with you knowing she was alone in another room of the house."

"We don't have to stay in the family house. We could build a house. You could be my wife in name only. You could...be with her there. It would be our secret."

Miss Kristian gasped and brought her fingers to her lips. "What are you saying?"

Mr. Stewart took her hand. "I understand these things because of my brother."

"The one who died?"

"Yes." Mr. Stewart looked away for a moment. "He was like you and Miss Rhona, and he died because of it."

Miss Kristian's eyes softened as she listened.

"I loved my brother. I always knew he was different. My parents wanted him to settle down with the daughter of a friend of theirs, but he tried to get away. He paid a man to smuggle him across the Mackinaw Bridge in a hidden compartment underneath the man's truck. They made it, but my brother died along the way of carbon monoxide poisoning. The man brought him back to us. It was very daring and he didn't have to do that. Before he left, my brother wrote me a note saying he hoped I understood what he was going to do. We told the Protectorate he committed suicide and we buried him on the hill in view of Canada."

"I'm so sorry! I didn't know."

"I still miss him. I don't fault him for wanting to be who he was, and I can't hold it against you and Miss Rhona. I'm trying to make it easier for you. I would do it for him."

"Mr. Stewart, you have your own life to live. You're doing this out of love because you are a wonderful man with a good heart. You think you won't mind, but you will. You deserve a woman who will be a real wife. Wait. I have something for you." She left and returned with the earrings. "You should take these. Give them to the woman you marry."

He opened the small box then snapped it shut. "What will you do?"

She paused, gazed out the window into the darkness, and turned to look him in the eye. "I'm leaving and I won't be back."

"You found a way. How?"

"It's better if you don't know."

"Then I pray for your safety. I won't say anything." He held the earring box in his right fist and punched his open palm.

"Then I'll request Miss Rhona," he stated. He sat up and became animated. "I'll find a way to get her to you. I can use these." He opened his fist to reveal the box.

Miss Kristian eyes widened. "You can get her to Canada?"

"Yes, I think so. With money you can do all kinds of things, even in the Protectorate. I'll retract my request for you and request her instead. I promise I'll get her to you. It might take a while. Or I could try to get you both out together, but that would take even longer."

"Miss Rhona will be of marrying age in March. You have to ask for her soon or else the Protectorate will assign her a husband."

"Someone must know about your plan. How will I find you?"

Miss Kristian considered his question. "The Porters will know. Please, don't say anything, not even to Miss Rhona. Not yet. Do you promise?"

"I won't tell anyone. After I amend my request, I'll arrange for Miss Rhona to move into my family home on the pretext of our marriage. After she's there, I'll tell her our plans. We won't ever marry. I'll get her out first, maybe in summer. You can trust me."

"I believe you, and I believe she'll trust you. She'll know you have good intentions. Tell me about Miss Rhona. How is she?"

"She's well, but she seems lonely. I never see her smile. She did have a visitor, a doctor."

"Hmm, that's probably Miss Analise's brother, Dr. Messer. I remember Miss Analise saying her brother was slow when it came to courting. He must still be interested. Take care of the paperwork. There's a chance Dr. Messer could request her first."

"I caught Mr. Kowalski looking in on her again and I told him to leave her alone. It's the strangest thing. He seems disgusted by her, he says nasty things, and yet he's fixated on her. Did you know we got into a fight over it?"

"I heard."

"Mr. Harlingen told me and Mr. Kowalski to keep our distance."

Mr. Browne and Mr. Porter made noise on the front porch to announce their arrival. They came in from the cold and knocked the snow from their boots.

"Did you two work it out?" asked Mr. Browne.

Miss Kristian smiled. "Yes. Everything's fine now. I should get started on dinner. You men must be hungry."

After the meal, Mr. Porter said he had to get Mr. Stewart back to the farm camp. They said their good-byes and Miss Kristian hugged Mr. Stewart on the way out.

"No hard feelings?" asked Mr. Browne after they left.

"He was good about it. It's over and I decided to give him the earrings. I'm ready to go with you to Canada, one hundred percent."

Chapter Fifteen

During her work at the feed mill, Miss Kristian thought of solutions to lighten the snowmobile. She made mental notes of removing metal from the frame or other fixes that would get them through the trip. They had to take fuel reserves. A five-hour trip might turn into seven or ten. She worried about the January thaw. Often times, the third or fourth week in January brought pleasant daytime temperatures. Harsh winter weather revisited in February, and by early March signs of spring would appear with crocuses popping their colorful heads up, sometimes through a couple of inches of snow. There hadn't been much new snow since the blizzard, though the cold temperatures remained. Each freezing night gave her more confidence they would make it.

Her concentration at church was no better. She prayed there would be no thaw this year. She prayed for snow and ice and more record-breaking cold. Miss Rhona had told her that a snowy winter would make it colder because sunlight would reflect instead of absorb into the ground. She prayed Miss Rhona was right.

Miss Kristian wanted to spend time fine-tuning the snowmobile engine and hoped to trim excess weight, but Mr. Porter said he had to drive up to Copper Harbor with her father to scope out potential launch sites. While they were away, she took out an old atlas and looked at the maps. In a few short weeks, she would call Canada her home.

Copper Harbor, at the northern tip of Superior Protectorate, was not too far from Marquette. Their ideal launch site would be just north of Hancock provided there was enough privacy. It would be foolish to call attention to their plan with a noisy engine after they had been so careful. The lakeshore was dotted with homes, but there were a few parks along the exposed shoreline where water levels had dropped. If they left in the wee hours, they would sneak away undetected. Mr. Porter wouldn't be implicated. He said he would bury all the extra snowmobile parts and keep nothing to remind him or anyone of what they had done. No one would suspect him of anything and he would say he didn't know what happened. She and her father would vanish. They would leave everything behind including the chips in their arms. They would disappear and in time, be forgotten.

Lake Superior, the largest of the Great Lakes, averaged five hundred feet deep and was over one thousand feet deep not far from where they lived. It was large enough to create its own tides and even in winter when ice formed over much of its surface, the sea churned and rolled. Large ships succumbed to its fury and the sea did not return its dead. These meant nothing to her now. She could visualize the lake as a vast white expanse with snow filling in crevasses, making for a long, smooth ride.

She moved her finger up the map to an island near the Canadian shore. Isle Royale National Park was now Isle Royale Provincial Nature Preserve and under Canadian authority as partial payment for damages caused during the war. It looked to be about sixty miles north-northwest of their starting point. The island was a long, thin strip inhabited by wolves. No humans would be there in the winter and Mr. Porter showed them where to skirt around it to the south and then head straight north. Heading west would land them in Minnesota and they might never get to Canada. If they hit questionable or open areas along their trip, Mr. Porter instructed them to travel due north. She traced her finger around the northern tip of Isle Royale to Thunder Bay, Ontario. They would turn west to reach it, adding a long detour she hoped to avoid.

The old map showed the approximate size and population of Thunder Bay. She had never been to a city larger than Marquette or Superior City, and she wondered how they would find their mother. Mr. Porter said she had settled in a small town called Neebing, south of Thunder Bay, but it wasn't on the map and she had no idea how far they might have to travel to get there. Perhaps Neebing had grown in twenty years or her mother may have moved on. She would find her somehow, or if they were turned over to the Canadian authorities, they could find her.

That night she slept fitfully. She woke to a darkened room. It was too early to rise. She fell back asleep and dreamt she, her father and Mr. Porter were driving in the van on the lake. They got out of the van and she could see Isle Royale. Dark spots formed on the shore and she heard the howl of wolves. Suddenly, she was at the shore. Though unseen, she knew the wolves were lurking behind the trees. She ran out on the lake to the van, took a shovel from the back and started digging a hole in the icy snow in which to protect herself. The snow had a wispy quality. It flew around and blinded her. The snow became gauze-like and she sensed her mother wrapped up in gauze below the surface, dead.

Miss Kristian opened her eyes and placed her hand over her pounding heart. A shred of reflected light illuminated the room. She lay in bed and thought about her dream. The covers kept her warm, maybe too warm. Beads of sweat lined the back of her neck. Her forehead felt warm, too. She wondered if she was sick, or perhaps the gravity of her adventure was sinking in—she could die.

It was not her day to work. She prepared breakfast while trying to shake her dizziness and her father took the community shuttle to the mill. While she was home mending a pair of his work slacks, she thought about packing up some of the items they would take and had already set aside: the compass, a silver-lined blanket, a tarp to cover the snowmobile, extra fuel, tool kit, and so on. Thinking about the tight helmet gave her a headache. How could she wear it for five hours, or six, or ten? They would have to bring food, but they didn't have to bring the camp stove. The Porters were used to camping and had equipment, sleeping bags, and more, but they needed to lighten their load, not increase it. Would they really need the ice saw?

She put away her lunch dishes and assembled bread-making ingredients. It crossed her mind to make sandwich rolls instead of a loaf, but that part would come after the bread rose. The sound of feet stomping at the front door got her attention. She dusted off her hands and her father walked in the door.

"You're home early."

"We have to go," he said. "Put that away and get your coat."

"I'm in the middle…."

"Don't argue with me! We're going."

His tone of voice scared her. She wiped her hands free of flour and set her bread bowl in the refrigerator. Behind her, she could hear him close the curtains. She donned her coat and they went outside where a light snow fell. She flashed back to her dream. In moments, Mr. Porter drove up and they got in the van. They drove in silence to Mr. Porter's house and she began to think the worst.

She went in and saw Mrs. Porter and Mr. Stewart sitting on the sofa.

"Miss Kristian." Mr. Stewart looked serious. He rose to greet her.

"What are you doing here?" she said. "I haven't been feeling well today and now I'm scared. Will someone please tell me what's going on?"

He turned his head and she followed his gaze to a woman standing in the hallway.

"Miss Rhona!"

She broke from his grasp and ran into Miss Rhona's arms. Miss Rhona cried and Miss Kristian could feel her body move with each sob. Tears fell while she hugged Miss Rhona with renewed strength.

"Miss Rhona," she cooed, "you're here, you're here."

"I missed you so much!"

"Come and sit," Mrs. Porter said. "I'll pour the tea."

"Did something happen?" Miss Kristian looked at the somber faces around the room. She sat next to Miss Rhona on the sofa. "Tell me!"

"I did what we talked about," Mr. Stewart said. "I went to the government office in Superior City and asked to amend my paperwork. They contacted me a couple of days later and said I didn't have to marry you, but I couldn't marry Miss Rhona."

Miss Kristian looked at Miss Rhona with questioning eyes.

"They said she had already been requested," Mr. Stewart continued. "I was too late."

"Oh." Miss Kristian pressed her lips together. "So Dr. Messer finally got around to it. I guess that changes everything."

"It was Mr. Kowalski," he said.

"WHAT? No! It can't be!"

Miss Rhona's lips quavered and she nodded her head. "I never would have known otherwise. They don't tell you. At least I found out."

"It can't happen! We can't let this happen!" Miss Kristian turned to Miss Rhona and held her. "We won't let it happen," she whispered. "We're here together again. We'll figure out something." She looked into Miss Rhona's eyes and felt love anew. She touched the soft skin on Miss Rhona's face and traced her red mark lovingly where it peeked above her sweater as she had done so many times before. She wanted everything and everyone to dissolve into nothingness so she could be alone with Miss Rhona and love her as they had in the past.

"I'm sorry," Mr. Stewart said. "I tried." He took a cup of tea from the tray Mrs. Porter offered and she set it down for the women to help themselves.

"That's why we're having this powwow," said Mr. Porter. "Miss Rhona is as good as done if we let her go with Mr. Kowalski. Not going to happen. She has no parents to protest his request. We have no choice but to take matters into our own hands."

"Do they know everything?" Miss Kristian asked Mr. Stewart.

"Yes. I had to tell them. I felt her life was at stake and I knew that was more important than keeping our secret. They told me the rest of the story, about your mother and the plans you've made with your father. We have to come up with a new plan to protect Miss Rhona."

Miss Kristian put her arm around Miss Rhona and breathed in her familiar scent. Memories flooded back and she drank them in. Miss Rhona's small frame seemed childlike and vulnerable. "We'll find a way. We will. We'll go into hiding. Father, you should take the snowmobile without me. Mr. Stewart can help us over the border. Do you think you can get us through Sault Saint Marie?"

"I don't know. I told you, these things take time."

"We don't have time," interjected Mr. Porter. "It's all well and good to say you'll go into hiding. Where will you do that? Under Mrs. Porter's bed? Think about it. You can say you're sick and miss a few days at the mill, but Miss Rhona will be missed tonight when she doesn't go back to the farm camp. Mr. Kowalski and everyone else will be asking about her."

"Miss Rhona could hide at our house," said Miss Kristian.

"That's the first place they'll look," her father said. "Mr. Porter, you know people. Isn't there someone, another Native American who would sympathize, who would take her in? We could remove Miss Rhona's chip. Then, they couldn't find her. It would buy us time while we figure out what to do."

"You would take out my chip?"

"Some folks saw us leave the camp. I'd have to say she ran away."

"Father, that's what you'll have to say about me."

"I'm not going anywhere, with or without you, until I know Miss Rhona is safe." Mr. Browne stroked his chin and addressed Mr. Porter. "What about your nephew in Superior City? Would he help?"

"Can't count on it. His wife has been in and out of the hospital."

"If they found me without my chip, you'd never hear from me again."

"They'd send you somewhere," Mr. Browne said. "I know this is all new to you Miss Rhona, but we've been planning for quite a while. Miss Kristian and I are prepared to remove our chips and make a run for it. We've committed."

"I can't tell you what it means to me that you planned to help me get away. Remember those times we planned to run away together?" Miss Rhona said to Miss Kristian. "We were going to fix up that old snowmobile we found at the cabin and drive it to Wisconsin." Miss Rhona smiled, but sadness played around her eyes.

"That's what you'll do," said Mr. Browne. "You'll take my place and the two of you will go together."

"There you go, talking nonsense again," Mr. Porter said. "How is Miss Kristian supposed to commandeer a snowmobile all the way to Thunder Bay when she's never so much as driven a van? On top of that, she's complaining like she's getting the flu."

"I have driven! Mr. Stewart let me drive on his property. But Father, you and I…"

"My daughter is more than capable. I say she takes my place. She can drive and Miss Rhona can sit in the back. There, it's done. We just dropped one hundred pounds of weight. You can do it. I believe in you. Are you feeling confident?"

"Yes! Miss Rhona, we'll do it. Please say you'll come with me."

Mr. Porter stomped his foot. "How can you send out these women by themselves? What about Miss Rhona's life?"

"My life is with Miss Kristian. And I would rather try to live with her and die with her, than accept my fate here. That to me would be death."

"Knowing Mr. Kowalski," said Mr. Stewart, "you may not be off the mark. I'll help you cross the border, Mr. Browne. We can come up with another plan and you can join them later."

"Great. It's settled," said Mr. Browne. "Let's get started. We have a lot of work to do. These two will be leaving tonight. I'm sure the battery has drained. Let's clip on the charger."

Miss Kristian hugged Miss Rhona. "We're going to do it and we're going to make it, I know it! Come into the workshop and see for yourself."

Miss Rhona was amazed at the work they had done. She ran her hand along the seat and touched the fuel tank. "This is what Mr. Porter did with the special biofuel I gave him. It's in here, isn't it?"

"And in there." Miss Kristian pointed to fuel containers they would take with them.

Mr. Browne ushered them aside and clipped on the battery charger cables. "This doesn't hold a charge for long. I hate to recommend this, but when you refuel, don't turn off the engine."

"Here, Miss Rhona. Try this on." Miss Kristian handed her the small helmet. It fit. Miss Kristian adjusted the chin strap and jiggled the helmet to see how much space there was underneath. "You'll need something else under here to stay warm. Did you bring extra clothes with you?"

"No. We left in a hurry. I didn't know what we were doing."

"We'll go back to our house to pick up clothes and the snowmobile suits. You can wear my father's. It'll be big. As long as you dress in layers, you should be okay. We'll need to pack food. Let's go in."

Mrs. Porter was busy in the kitchen and she shooed them away when they tried to help. "You should nap while you have the chance. You'll be up all night. Miss Kristian, you look a bit peaked."

"I didn't sleep well."

"Then sleep now. Go on."

They went into the bedroom and took off their jackets. There was only one bedroom in the small house with a double bed where the Porter's slept. Miss Kristian closed the door. They stripped to their thermals and got under the covers.

"I can't believe I'm with you again," said Miss Kristian as she leaned over Miss Rhona. "I've missed you so much."

"I've missed you, too. I've been lonely without you, like a part of me was missing."

Miss Kristian stroked Miss Rhona's face and kissed her lightly. The feel of her lips was like heaven. She kissed her over and over.

Miss Rhona smiled and held her close. "I've never been in a bed this big. I wish it was ours."

"We'll have our own bed someday and it will be this big or bigger!"

Miss Kristian rested on her side and bent her knees so they could spoon. It was hot with the two of them under the covers, and she flipped off a blanket. The two settled in again and soon Miss Kristian was asleep with her arms around her love.

She awoke in darkness and felt disoriented. Remembering where she was, she reached for Miss Rhona, but found only a warm depression where she had lain. The back of her neck felt moist and she flapped the covers to bring in cooler air. Instead of feeling rested, she felt fatigued. Voices carried from the other part of the house. She roused herself, cracked the door ajar to let in light, and put on her clothes.

Miss Kristian shielded her eyes from the light as she entered the living area. Miss Rhona took her hand and they joined the others at the table. Dinner had already been served. Mrs. Porter filled a bowl with chili and grated cheese on top.

"We didn't want to wake you," said Miss Rhona. "They told me we'll be awake all night and that you need your strength."

"Eat, dear," said Mrs. Porter. "It will be the last hot food you'll have for a while."

"What about the camp stove?"

"Decided to leave it here," Mr. Porter said. "This isn't a picnic. You'll carry your food inside your snowsuit to keep it from freezing. We're packing two tall thermoses with hot chicken broth."

"Everything's in the van," her father said. "We went back to the house while you were asleep and I took your clothes. We'll sort through them before we head out."

"When will we leave?"

"Soon."

"We've been waiting for you to wake up," said Mr. Stewart. "It's almost ten o'clock."

"Ten o'clock!" Miss Kristian felt flushed. She touched her damp forehead with her napkin.

"You're sick, aren't you?" said Mr. Porter. "Well, how's that for timing?"

Mrs. Porter placed her hand across Miss Kristian's forehead. "A little warm, is all."

"I'm okay. I'm just nervous. I'll be fine."

Mrs. Porter looked worried. "After you finish here, I'm going to take the chip out."

Miss Rhona pushed up her sleeve. "Look." Her forearm was wrapped in white gauze. A bloody circle marked the spot. "I did it. It's gone. It's hard to explain, but it feels wonderful."

Miss Kristian felt a wave of nausea and swallowed. She put down her spoon. Had she known, she might have chosen to have the chip removed before she ate. She closed her eyes, took a deep breath, opened her eyes and smiled. "I'm ready. Let's do it."

"I had Mr. Porter sharpen my good fillet knife. It has the finest blade. Mr. Stewart, will you get the ice?"

Mrs. Porter cleared an area on the kitchen table. Miss Kristian took off her sweater, rolled up her outer flannel shirt sleeve, and pushed her thermal layer to her elbow. She felt the chip beneath her skin as she had many times during her life. It was part of her. Mrs. Porter palpated her tendon. She nodded to Mr. Stewart who looked serious as he held the ice against her skin. Miss Kristian felt nervous with everyone looking on, but then she felt a shift. She looked at each of them one at a time in the brightly lit kitchen and felt supported. They loved her, each in their own way, and they were committed to her future.

"Shall we hold her down," asked Mr. Porter.

"No," Miss Kristian said. "I can take it."

"They held me," Miss Rhona said. "I think it helped."

"No, I'm fine. The ice is starting to make my skin hurt."

"That's a good sign. Stay with it a little longer."

The ice turned her skin red. Cold drops ran off the side of her arm as the ice melted and the area felt of pins and needles. Miss Kristian signaled she was ready. Mrs. Porter washed her hands. She held the knife blade over the stove flame and then let it cool. She wiped off a blackened area from the blade with a clean towel. Then she did the same with a pair of tweezers. She nodded and Mr. Stewart took away the ice. Mrs. Porter placed the towel on the table top and rested Miss Kristian's forearm over it. She blotted off the moisture, opened a bottle of iodine and ran the applicator tip over the area, coating it with the translucent brown liquid. She gave it a moment to dry.

"Don't move and don't make a fist. It's probably encapsulated, like Miss Rhona's, but if there's scar tissue, we'll have to cut around."

She felt for the chip with the tip of the blade and then pierced her skin. Miss Kristian sucked in her breath. Blood ran down her wrist. Mrs. Porter sliced in deeper and Miss Kristian took a stronger breath. She grimaced in pain and bared her teeth.

"Almost there."

Mr. Stewart picked up the tweezers and handed them to Mrs. Porter. Miss Kristian closed her eyes. Pain seared up her arm as Mrs. Porter dug out the chip. She could feel the extra pressure of the tweezers and heard them snap as they slipped off a couple of times. Jabbing pain coursed through her as she felt the tip of the knife again cutting into her tissues. She splayed her fingers and saw red beneath her eyelids.

"Got it!"

She opened her eyes and saw the bloodied shape of the chip next to the tweezers while Mrs. Porter pressed a wadded piece of gauze over the wound and wrapped tight circles of gauze around her arm to hold it in place.

"Good girl," Mrs. Porter said. "Put pressure on this until the bleeding stops. Too bad I don't have an infirmary here like at the farm camp. I wish I had some tape."

"It hurts, but I feel adrenaline rushing through me."

"Keep breathing steady. We'll give it a bit of time. Then I'll put on a butterfly and we'll wrap it again."

"You were very brave," said Mr. Browne, "though I thought Mr. Stewart might pass out!"

Everyone laughed.

Mr. Stewart's ears flushed red. "I wanted to help."

"You've helped more than you'll ever know," Miss Kristian said.

"Now, you rest for a moment on the sofa with your head propped and your arm up, and I'll check on you in a moment." Mrs. Porter removed the blood stained towel to the sink and Miss Kristian did as she was told.

Miss Rhona and Mr. Stewart joined her in the living area.

"You should meet Miss Chastity," Miss Kristian said to Mr. Stewart. "She's one of the nicest people you'll ever know." "And a great cook," added Miss Rhona.

"I know who you mean. I've seen her," said Mr. Stewart. "It might take me a while to think about someone else."

"Get to know her," Miss Kristian said, "and love her for who she is. She'll make a fine wife."

Miss Kristian felt woozy and closed her eyes. Her arm

throbbed and her fingers felt numb. She rested quietly while Miss Rhona stroked her hair and the voices of the people she loved faded away.

Chapter Sixteen

"**M**iss Kristian, Miss Kristian," said Mrs. Porter. "Wake up, now. You need to get going. You have a big adventure ahead of you."

"I must have nodded off," she said.

"I need to see your incision. Mr. Porter found the tape."

Mrs. Porter cleaned her wound and redressed it, using sticky bandages to close the cut. "This won't win any beauty contests, but it's all we could find." She cut a piece of gray duct tape from a roll. Miss Rhona held a thick gauze square in place while Mrs. Porter laid down strips of tape to secure the bandage to Miss Kristian's arm.

Mr. Browne retrieved several bags of clothing and the two women went into the bedroom and tried on pieces to decide on the best layering method. Miss Rhona changed out of her dress and into layers of thermals, flannels, sweaters, overalls, and the snowsuit. Miss Kristian did the same until she could hardly move. The sleeves on Miss Rhona's suit went beyond her hands and for the moment, Miss Kristian folded them up. Rather quickly, Miss Kristian felt a heat wave and removed all but the basic layers.

Miss Rhona pulled something out of her bag. "This is for you." She handed Miss Kristian a piece of folded paper.

She smiled "It's the photo of my mother."

"She looks like you. I carried it with me."

"Thank you." She hugged Miss Rhona and put the photograph in her overalls.

They went outside to the workshop. Light snow continued to fall and had accumulated about two inches since it started earlier in the day. The snowmobile was already loaded into the van, as was the extra fuel and the survival packages the men assembled. Miss Kristian gave Miss Rhona the small helmet and she took the large one for herself. The men showed them where everything was packed. Mr. Porter handed a compass to Miss Kristian. He had attached it to a chain and he clipped it to her overalls like an old pocket watch. It was time.

As she sat in the van holding Miss Rhona's hand, she reflected back on their good-byes. Mr. Stewart's eyes had gotten round and moist in a way she had never seen. Mrs. Porter had not held back her tears and insisted Miss Kristian eat a few more bites before leaving. She was as close to a mother as any woman had been and those tender moments were imprinted forever in her memory.

Mr. Porter drove north of Houghton. The snow came down more heavily and he turned on the van's wipers. At Calumet, he turned east off the highway and then south along Lake Shore Drive. He pulled over at a turnout, with his headlights shining onto the lake. Miss Kristian had never been through the area, which was much like the shore at Marquette. She remembered the lake in summer with its sparkling water, and how the stiff wind blew the waves into whitecaps that peaked and disappeared.

Mr. Porter turned off the engine. "This is it. Put on your clothes." He turned on the overhead light and they dressed. Miss Kristian felt for the photo in her right pocket and the compass in her left. She pulled on her suit and gloves, and moved to the rear of the vehicle to help the men. She helped steady the machine as they rolled it down a ramp out the rear doors. She felt warm in her layered clothing and stood while the men strapped everything on the snowmobile.

They pushed the snowmobile down a gradual slope where the water line had receded over the years. Her boots squeaked in the fresh snow. Larger flakes were forming, and as they floated to the ground they seemed to absorb all the sounds around them.

"I love you, father," she said as she hugged him.

He held her tightly and brushed away her tears. "No crying. They'll freeze," he said. "I love you, too. I'll be seeing you and your mother soon. I know it."

Miss Kristian hugged Mr. Porter.

"I can't thank you enough," she said. "In my heart you're family, and I'll always remember you."

"Just remember everything I told you. You can start by taking out your compass."

Miss Rhona expressed her gratitude and said her good-byes. The four of them held hands in a circle and Mr. Porter said an old Indian prayer for safe travel. They bowed their heads in silent prayer and when they were through they squeezed hands and let go.

The women put on their balaclavas, coverings that fit snugly over their heads and faces with a wide oval cut-out for the eyes. Mr. Browne helped his daughter with her helmet and Mr. Porter did the same for Miss Rhona. Miss Kristian mounted the snowmobile and Mr. Porter half-lifted Miss Rhona in place behind her.

"Hold on like your life depends on it. And no fancy turns."

She turned on the headlamp, then the key, and pressed the starter. It turned several times and caught.

"God's speed," Mr. Porter said.

Mr. Browne gave his daughter a pat on the shoulder; she turned the throttle and headed into the night.

She was glad they had found a smooth launch area. The headlights of the van beaming out ahead of them became faint and in no time disappeared altogether, leaving the dull glow of the snowmobile headlight. It seemed to brighten as she got used to the dark, but did not cast its light very far in front of them. She turned and saw the van drive down the highway. It would be too risky for the men to linger and she prayed the snowy weather kept anyone from seeing them or hearing the snowmobile engine. She guessed it was around two a.m. Any person in their right mind would be asleep in their bed.

She backed off on the throttle as they passed over a series of bumps and then brought it up to speed at sixteen miles per hour. Miss Rhona held her tightly around the waist. She hit a second set of bumps, mounds like miniature low rolling hills and these she traversed with ease.

Traveling on the snowmobile was not as she had imagined. It wasn't like the all-terrain vehicle she and Mr. Stewart had ridden at his family farm with its big knobbed tires, which had felt light in comparison. She understood now why Mr. Porter said the snowmobile was like pulling a plow. The chain underneath their seat trudged along like a reluctant mule.

It was hard to tell if the snow was still falling or if a breeze had picked up the light snow and was now blowing it around. It came directly at her. Mr. Porter had warned them that once on the lake the wind would increase. Sourced from the northwest and with ninety miles of flat lake surface, the wind would garner enough force to slow them down.

She was not used to the steady vibration of the snowmobile and she alternately relaxed her grip and made it tighter. Her arm ached where Mrs. Porter had removed her chip. It would heal. In a week it would be scabbed over. In a month, only a line would remain, a scar to remind her, not that she would ever forget.

Snow danced around in front of the snowmobile in patterns that formed and disappeared. She caught herself looking at them and realized she had turned. She straightened out and thought it best to check her compass. She stopped and held the item in front of her. It was too dark to see.

"Where's your mini-light?" she asked Miss Rhona.

Miss Rhona rustled behind her and shone a light over her shoulder. They were pointed too far north. Miss Kristian lurched ahead a few feet while turning the handlebars. They felt stiff. When she was satisfied they were back on track, she opened up the throttle and stayed at her designated speed.

She had no conception of time and though they had talked about taking a watch, their hurried departure made it one more thing forgotten. One minute was the same as the next. Her task was to stay focused, keep the steering straight, don't push the engine. Mr. Porter had been instructive on many points, and she tried to remember them all by replaying them. Knowing she was responsible for their safety helped keep her alert.

Miss Rhona held tight. She wanted to talk to her companion, touch her face, and feel her body in the warmth of a bed. Miss Rhona's arms tight around her waist were assurance enough that those moments would come to pass again. Conversation would come later as would time to be alone together. She felt sorry for other women like her, women who loved other women, and for the men who loved men. It was by chance they were born into Superior Protectorate. Surely there were others like her who escaped. Perhaps she would meet them in Canada.

Miss Rhona tapped Miss Kristian. She released the throttle and coasted to a stop. Miss Rhona indicated she had to relieve herself, not an easy task. Miss Rhona was wearing Mr. Browne's suit. She would need to remove it to do her business. The wind was mild, but she squatted next to the snowmobile to use it as a windbreak. Miss Kristian decided to go, too. They sipped a small amount of hot chicken broth and remounted.

They would continue on, follow Mr. Porter's instructions and everything would be fine. It was a matter of waiting, waiting while riding. She rode over another series of bumps and imagined them as waves far beneath the surface. It flattened out and she came upon a larger set. These, too, she crossed without difficulty.

Miss Kristian could only see what was in front of her and supposed everything to either side must be the same. The snow had stopped falling, but the wind became stronger. It blew snow at her and though she was protected by the windshield and helmet, she could feel it on her legs and arms. Her left arm ached badly and she wished she could control the snowmobile with one hand, but Mr. Porter had warned against that practice. She could feel the wind press against the snowmobile like an unseen hand thwarting their progress.

The monotonous scene was at times hypnotic and played tricks with her eyes. She imagined weaving her way through high mountains of ice. She felt she was cruising down a river of ice, floating along, and then a bumpy ride would shake her back into reality. She felt as if she was not driving on a flat surface, but actually heading upward and down. There was no distant horizon to check where she was and it helped to imagine a flat surface so as not to become disoriented.

After a while, she was sure she was not imagining this effect because she detected a change in the engine sound as she rose and fell. She listened carefully and wondered if Miss Rhona could tell the difference. She let off the throttle and twisted her body around when they stopped.

"Did you feel that?" she asked over the loud idle.

"What?"

"The bumps."

"Yes."

"Where's the big flashlight?"

"In the back."

Miss Kristian stepped off the snowmobile. The wind hit Miss Rhona who hunkered down to protect herself. Miss Kristian stood up to the powerful wind. She felt stiff and rolled her shoulders as much as she could. She found the flashlight and flipped it on.

Ahead was a towering wall of ice. To the right, left, and behind, giant iceberg-like blocks jutted upward as though angry gods had thrown down huge icicles that broke apart and froze in place.

"What is this?" Miss Rhona yelled.

"Look around," she said while shining the light on the obstacles before them. "Mr. Porter warned about this. Agh! We have to go back and then drive around. We can't get through here! I can't believe I'm in this far. The headlight is so weak I couldn't tell."

"Don't panic. Let's turn around. I'll shine the flashlight in front of you. Will that help?"

"I don't know. Maybe if we go slowly I can retrace our tracks."

"Hurry. The snow is already starting to cover them up."

Miss Kristian turned a tight circle and retraced her route. In moments their former tracks were covered with blowing snow. She kept her steering straight to head out safely. She had Miss Rhona shine the flashlight, but it was of no use. The blowing snow made visibility impossible. All they could see were flecks of white blowing sideways in the darkness. She remembered the rolling feel before entering and when the rolls were less pronounced, she told Miss Rhona they would head north.

At brief moments, the blowing slowed and she could see more than a few feet ahead. She crept forward at barely above an idle. At five miles per hour, it hardly seemed worth the effort, yet going faster would mean driving blind. She feared she would come upon another towering mountain of white, but she did not share her thoughts. She would get them to Canada, even if it took ten hours.

She motored onward. Though the snowy ride was flat, she was uncertain about what they might encounter. Feeling Miss Rhona's arms around her waist made her feel competent, as if Miss Rhona had no doubts about their ultimate arrival. With patience, the shoreline would come into view. Perhaps they would see mountains or other land features first. They would see activity and motor in to a spot where they would likely be received.

As they traveled north, the wind blew at them from the left side, pushing like a cold hand through the insulation in her snowsuit. Miss Kristian could tell Miss Rhona had tucked her head low to protect herself. The windshield was useless. There was no effective way to fight the wind. Her sore left arm ached horribly from holding on. Visibility was reduced to a few feet and she slowed their speed, knowing it would take longer to reach their destination.

Crunch! The front end lurched up and the snowmobile came to an abrupt stop. Miss Rhona bumped into Miss Kristian's backside.

"What happened?"

Miss Kristian could see nothing in front of them, but it was obvious they were tilted upward. "Get out the flashlight!"

Using Miss Kristian to steady herself, Miss Rhona got off the snowmobile and retrieved the light. They had climbed a short ridge. In front of them, a giant wall of ice thrust up from the lake's snowy surface, providing a wind break.

"Oh, no," Miss Rhona said. "I hope we're not stuck. What should we do?"

Miss Kristian thought a moment. "I think we should stay here until dawn." She turned off the snowmobile. In the rear compartment, she took out a sleeping bag, the aluminum blanket and tarp. She walked a few feet and found a hollowed out area in the wall of ice. She motioned for Miss Rhona to follow her. The carved out area was better protected from the direct wind, though snow circled inside the cavity. She stood on the tarp, unzipped the sleeping bag and placed their aluminum blanket beneath it.

"Leave your helmet on."

They both got in the sleeping bag, boots, helmets and all. It could not be zipped. Miss Kristian turned her back to the open end.

"Help me roll."

Miss Kristian held one end of the tarp and they rolled over twice. They held one another in silence and waited. In the relative quiet, she could hear the snow hit against the icy backdrop. Her helmet shield fogged up and feared ice crystals would form on the inside, even though she was warm. She was almost too warm, at least her front where she met Miss Rhona. Her backside began to feel the cold and after a time, she turned her back toward the inside. She repeated this process several times. Miss Rhona did not move, nor did she speak. Miss Kristian knew she was reserving her resources for the rest of the trip.

Though Miss Kristian did not believe she slept, she fell into a dream state. Strange images floated before her and then vanished or morphed into other shapes before she could focus on them. She heard someone calling from a distance, or a sound like an owl, she thought, and there were scratching noises similar to the branch against her window at home. These all faded when she opened her eyes.

In the darkness, she detected a strange calm. The wind had died. There was no swirling snow or scratching noises. The cold penetrated the muscles of her back and she shivered inside the bedroll. She stifled a sneeze and then another. She turned to warm her back against Miss Rhona. The warmth she had felt earlier when switching sides did not come. Her whole body felt cold and she stiffened with every minute.

She shook violently, trying to cast off the spell.

"Are you okay?" Miss Rhona asked.

Miss Kristian opened her eyes and saw a line of light extending from the horizon. The sun would be up soon. Yellow-pink tinges spread across the sky and she saw a small yellow bead rise above the horizon line.

"The sun's coming up. We should go."

"I'm hungry," said Miss Rhona.

"Me, too. I'm very cold."

"My feet are cold. My neck is cold."

Miss Kristian turned her body and they unrolled themselves out of the aluminum blanket and tarp. The hard ice felt bruising and she sat up. No wind pushed against them, but it took effort to move her stiff body.

"I feel sick," Miss Kristian said. "I need some broth, but first I have to start up the snowmobile. The battery doesn't hold a charge very long."

There was a little bit of light, enough to see their environment. They had stopped in between mountains of ice. The front skis were partially buried in the ridge that stopped their progress and Miss Kristian hoped nothing was damaged.

She scraped the frost covered dials with the sharp edges of her gloved fingertips and freed up the key, which she had left in place overnight. She sat down, turned the key, and pushed the starter. The engine began to turn over, but did not catch. She tried again, and when the turning sound slowed she stopped. The engine sounds were not encouraging. It was hard to think. In her mind, she heard Mr. Porter instructing her. The headlight! She had forgotten to get the juice going by first turning on the headlight. This she did. She held her breath while praying in the few seconds before she pressed the starter. It turned and caught. She exhaled and a wave of emotion sent a tear from her eye. She brushed her thick glove against the dial showing how much fuel was left. There was about a third of a tank, not low enough to refuel. She could not remember the odometer reading from the previous evening. She calculated they had gone about forty miles, though she had no idea how far off course they had driven. She turned the throttle to warm the engine and let it idle.

Miss Rhona folded up the aluminum blanket and tarp, and put them away. She motioned for Miss Kristian to join her in their carved out cubby to eat. They removed their helmets. Miss Rhona poured her a cup of chicken broth. Miss Kristian edged her balaclava below her lips to drink. The broth was warm and felt good going down. Her nose ran and she wiped it with her sleeve.

"You have a cold, don't you?" Miss Rhona said.

Miss Kristian nodded.

"Eat."

Miss Rhona reached inside her snowsuit and retrieved a smashed chicken sandwich. She took small bites and washed it down with the broth that had chilled in the cup. She ate faster.

Miss Kristian ate her sandwich, but her hunger faded before she finished. Her arm had a powerful ache and it took effort to bring the sandwich to her mouth. Miss Rhona encouraged her to eat more.

"We have the rest of our adventure ahead of us. You must feed your body."

Miss Kristian responded to this encouragement and finished her sandwich. It had been wrapped in corn paper, which she folded and put in her pocket. In an emergency, she could eat that, too.

The sun had risen and the ice mountains surrounding them cast long shadows.

"It's beautiful!" Miss Kristian said. "It's like nothing I've ever seen. These spires have to be twenty feet tall. Taller!"

"Thirty!"

"These forms are so graceful," she pointed where they had rested. "How does that happen?"

"It's the wind," Miss Rhona said. "The snow and wind carve out these shapes. We're the only ones who will ever see them. In spring the sun will melt all of this back into Lake Superior."

Miss Rhona stood and marveled at the sight. She put away the thermos and helped Miss Kristian break the ice away from the skis so they could begin their journey. The left ski was cracked and wobbled inside the metal frame holding it in place. It could break away and not deter their progress.

Miss Kristian found the morning light reassuring, as she could now rely on her sight to help them find their way. She reversed the snowmobile back off the ridge and turned the steering. It was stiffer than she remembered. Her arm ached anew as she used her strength to turn the handlebars. Miss Rhona got on, settled herself, and then Miss Kristian headed north away from the ice chunks that had impeded their progress. The snowmobile veered to the right and she had to push to the left to keep it straight. Something had gone out of alignment when she hit the ridge.

To their right the lake was flat and she ventured in that direction to take advantage of a smoother ride. As they rode, up ahead she could see what looked to be smaller hills of ice. The farther they traversed, the smaller the chunks rose up out of the lake until they passed the fearsome teeth of ice that could have caused their undoing the previous evening.

The sun's rise made for intense brightness as rays bounced off the white landscape. She stopped the snowmobile and the two put on their sunglasses. She held her compass out to get her bearings headed north-northwest. There was no land in sight. Turning the throttle, she found her top speed of eighteen miles per hour and held tight.

Vibration from the snowmobile seemed to bring her senses

into awareness. Her head felt woozy and the helmet felt heavier than the previous evening. Even with the sunglasses, a dizzying array of colors sparkled in her vision. The bright light made her squint, but it wasn't enough to keep her eyes from tearing. She continued on and when the fuel gauge dropped low, she stopped.

"Let's add fuel," she said, "before we run out."

The women unstrapped one of the extra fuel containers. It felt light to Miss Kristian. She opened it to find it was half full.

"Our fuel!"

"Pour in what's left," Miss Rhona said.

Miss Kristian lifted the seat. It took all her strength to screw off the fuel cap. She poured in the fuel, about one gallon, and held the container up to see the problem. She noted a tiny crack and tossed the canister aside.

"We might as well go for it before anything else happens."

They unstrapped the second fuel container and poured in the entire two gallons. She set it aside, closed the fuel cap and flipped the seat back in place. It was all the fuel they had, enough to get them to Canada should nothing else go wrong.

"Do you want me to take over?" Miss Rhona asked.

"Do you think you can? You have to be strong. The steering is pulling hard to the right. I could use a break."

"I'll go slowly. Slow and steady. That's how we'll get there, slow and steady."

She showed Miss Rhona what to do by reaching around her and pointing at the controls. When she felt Miss Rhona had a feel for the machine, she held on around Miss Rhona's middle. For the next hour, they cruised smoothly at ten to fifteen miles an hour. During that time, there was very little change in the landscape. The sun continued to rise through a cloudless sky and the wind picked up again blowing straight toward them. Miss Rhona seemed sufficiently protected by the front windshield, but Miss Kristian, who sat up higher on the rear seat, could feel the force coming at her. She kept her head down as much as possible, but found it a difficult position to maintain. Her entire body ached and the weight of the helmet was becoming unbearable. She tapped on Miss Rhona's leg and the snowmobile cruised to a stop. She explained her problem to Miss Rhona and the two decided to take a small break. They finished off the contents of the first thermos and started on the second.

Feeling somewhat refreshed, Miss Kristian resumed driving. She was glad the night was over. Impatient to see land, she imagined the elation she would feel upon their arrival. Surely, they would see land soon. She tried to push their speed to twenty to make up for lost time, but when she hit a bump, the broken front left ski flew off and narrowly missed her head. She stopped and pointed at the frame with its missing ski. Miss Rhona nodded, but said nothing as she pointed forward.

Fresh snow blew across the horizon creating an effect similar to dense fog. A cloud of white hugging the ground stretched out on all sides. Visibility was poor. Fortunately, the sun and snow-glare was behind them—a small comfort.

Above the layer of white blowing snow, she could see blue sky. Its crisp aqua color was deepened by her sunglasses. Looking up helped prevent snow blindness. Peering ahead made her feel confident about avoiding obstacles that sprang up from time to time.

She peered at the sky and noticed a darker edge above the horizon. It disappeared into the blowing sea of white and reappeared. At first, she thought she might be imagining her destination, a mirage in the distance, but during moments when the wind slowed, there was no doubt. Land! There was land straight ahead. She excitedly tapped Miss Rhona to get her attention and stopped the snowmobile. She pointed ahead and Miss Rhona registered her excitement by wiggling a dance. She hugged Miss Kristian.

"There it is! I knew we could do it!"

Miss Kristian raised her arms in victory and dropped them. Searing pain shot through her left arm. She hoped Miss Rhona's wound was not as painful. Determined to end their odyssey, she settled into position with her hands on the grips and turned the throttle.

As they neared land, tall white spruce came into sharper view. They were beautiful and towered over other pines. Their dark boughs were layered in white snow. Next, she identified the smaller black spruce. Excitement coursed through her. Soon. She watched for cabins and other signs of habitation, but saw none. She assumed this was Isle Royale, which stretched for almost fifty miles. They had traveled north and east during their nighttime and morning drive, and now she would have to continue northeast to round the tip of the island. It was a longer route and at this point, the only choice. The island loomed large. Its thick stands of pines and uncertain hills would make crossing over land a mistake. She was better off traveling on the smooth surface of the lake, even though it was farther.

She continued on until she saw what appeared to be a break. The island ended and a small string of islands lay farther north. She turned westward and imagined the map in the atlas. They were entering Thunder Bay. If they had the good fortune of coming in from the south end, they would have been fifteen miles from land. Coming from the north, it would be longer, twenty-five miles or so in all. She wasn't sure of the exact number, but knew they were close. It was an important milestone. If she had to walk the rest of the way, she would do it. They were going to make it.

Rolling mounds of surface ice reminded her of the same formations they encountered the previous evening when they left the landing off Superior Protectorate. It seemed a lifetime ago. They had been on the snowmobile for hours. She wanted nothing more than to soak in a warm bath to relieve her body aches. She sneezed. Moisture from her nose ran into her balaclava. She could taste it. Her sinuses were stuffed and her head ached from the heavy helmet. Pain between her eyes spread to her face. She couldn't take it any longer. She stopped the snowmobile and handed her helmet to Miss Rhona.

"Are you sure?" Miss Rhona asked. "I could drive again."

"No. Hold it for me. Put it between your legs or something. Just for a while."

"I'm afraid your head will get cold. I'm hot and cold."

"My feet are freezing."

"My knees are cold."

Miss Kristian wiped her nose on her sleeve. Cold air on her head filtering through her balaclava felt refreshing and perked her up. She opened the top vee of her snowsuit before starting off again. Without her helmet, she felt a new sense of freedom. Cold air filtered down the back of her neck and chilled the sweaty area down her back. It felt good in a way, but after half an hour she questioned the wisdom of her decision. Soon they would see the city; she was sure of it. If the wind would only stop blowing, Canada would come into their sights. They couldn't be far away. Her teeth began to chatter and the tip of her nose lost its feeling, but her body felt too hot. She couldn't imagine zipping her suit, so she continued on.

The lake was flat and the going easy. She clenched her jaw so her teeth wouldn't chatter, but it was useless. Without her helmet, cold surrounded her head. In a short time, it felt like tiny needles were pressing into her scalp and ears. Soon. They should see land soon, if only the wind would stop. If only they could see ahead. If only it didn't feel as if the moisture on her eyes was freezing. She squinted her eyes into tiny slits. Tears ran out to the sides of her head and she felt them freeze onto her balaclava.

She couldn't see anything now. She tried to keep her speed steady, but didn't know for sure how fast she was going. Everything was a blur. She wiped away the wetness and before her was land—massive, broad, and dark behind a film of snow. She turned up the throttle and sped ahead. After a short time, her engine protested, but she didn't care. The engine coughed roughly; the snowmobile alternately ran in bursts and then lagged. She gave it a little more throttle, but there was no more speed to be had. The engine died and they coasted to a stop.

Now there was no doubt. The great land of Canada was before them. The sight of it made her cry. She turned to Miss Rhona and suggested she remove her helmet, which Miss Rhona did. They got off the snowmobile and hugged.

"We made it! We made it!" Miss Rhona cried. "I love you and now we'll be together forever!"

"And I love you!" Miss Kristian shouted in a raspy voice that caught on the wind. They kissed and held one another, then turned to see land before them. Wind shifts made their destination blur and magically reappear. It was hard to say how many miles they were from shore. Three? Five? Ten?

Miss Kristian lifted the seat and removed the fuel cap, though she knew they had run out of fuel. She put the cap back on and shook her head, her teeth chattering uncontrollably.

"Before we do another thing," Miss Rhona said, "you need to get warm."

She got out the aluminum blanket, tarp, sleeping bag, and thermos, and poured Miss Kristian a cup of broth. It had lost much of its warmth, but it would provide nourishment.

"Drink this," she encouraged Miss Kristian. "You're probably dehydrated."

Miss Rhona drank next, then capped off the small amount left. She guided Miss Kristian to the right side of the snowmobile where it might have been a little less windy. She opened the sleeping bag, zipped her in, and tucked the aluminum blanket and tarp around her. Miss Rhona ate a small bite of food as she sat a vigil.

Miss Kristian was in no shape to digest food, even the soup, which should have given her some comfort. Instead, she felt queasy and curled into a fetal position. She protested when Miss Rhona told her to remove her clothes down to her thermals.

"Trust me," Miss Rhona said. "I'm going to get in there with you. My body heat will help warm you up. Give me your snowsuit. We'll put it beneath the sleeping bag."

Miss Kristian did as she was told. Next, Miss Rhona told her to stuff her clothes into the bottom of the bag. Miss Rhona quickly got out of her clothes and held them as she climbed into the sleeping bag, positioning her snowsuit on top of them. She had tucked an edge of the aluminum blanket beneath Miss Kristian and they rolled together face-to-face to form a cocoon.

In a short time, Miss Kristian stopped shivering. Her breathing became deeper, her muscles relaxed and her queasiness dissipated.

"It's working. You've warmed up. How's your arm?"

"It's okay, but I'm afraid you're going to catch my cold."

"So? At least we're going to live. We're going to live in Canada! Are you ready?"

"Yes!" Miss Kristian kissed her. "You are my love and my life, and I will always be with you."

"And you are my love and my life, and I will always be with you, and care for you, and never leave you—ever! Let's go!"

They rolled in reverse to unwrap their bundle. Miss Rhona

jumped out and quickly put on her clothes and helmet. Miss Kristian put her layers on inside the sleeping bag. She crawled out to put on her snowsuit and helmet.

"Let's figure out what to take," Miss Rhona said.

"Only the food. We can come back for this later."

Miss Rhona insisted that Miss Kristian finish the last of the broth. They secured the thermos with their other belongings onto the snowmobile and headed out on foot.

Snow crunched beneath their boots. The shore called to them and although they could imagine making a run for it, they proceeded at a slow pace to conserve their energy, as the shore was miles away. As the sun rose higher, reflected light made shadows deceptive. The surface of the lake was not always smooth and both of them tripped from time to time over jutting chunks of ice. They took two short breaks in the first hour, nibbling on a little dried fruit. Excitement and determination got them back on their feet.

As they trudged on, Miss Kristian thought her eyes were playing tricks on her. Colorful dots appeared on the ice, and unlike her earlier snow blindness, the dots were stationary and got larger as they approached.

"Do you see those things?" she asked Miss Rhona. "They're like gumdrops."

"I think they're shacks for ice-fishing."

"Couldn't be; that would be illegal."

"We're not in the Protectorate anymore."

The women faced one another and shouted in unison, "We're not in the Protectorate anymore!"

Miss Kristian took Miss Rhona's hand and ran toward the nearest one, a green wooden shack. They stumbled and slowed to a manageable jog.

"We're here!" Miss Kristian shouted when they reached the shack. "Hey! Anyone there?" She ran ahead. "Hello?" She pounded on the shack. The door handle was locked and it was obviously empty inside. "Come on," she waved to Miss Rhona. "We need to keep going."

None of the other shacks had snowmobiles next to them, so they headed toward land. After another half hour, buildings on the shore came into focus and they discussed what they would do first and say to the people they met. The area reminded them of their homeland. Cottages lined the shoreline. Cars passed along roads. Perhaps being in Canada wouldn't be so different.

Miss Kristian felt excitement build as she and Miss Rhona chose a likely place to go ashore, a dock leading to what could have been a lodge or restaurant. It was all she could do to keep from running, but it was more important to be at Miss Rhona's side when they stepped foot on land. Miss Rhona picked up her pace and the next thing she knew, they were both racing toward the dock.

Miss Kristian grabbed the metal railing of a ladder leading up from the ice and climbed up. She extended her hand to help Miss Rhona onto the dock. They embraced, exhausted. Miss Kristian removed her helmet and Miss Rhona did the same.

"We made it!" Miss Kristian cried.

"I'm so happy!" Miss Rhona replied.

They hugged and dried their tears. Leaving their helmets on the dock, they ran to the entrance of the brick building and tried the door. It was locked, but they saw two women inside a second enclosed entryway cleaning a wooden banister. They pounded on the door until one of them took notice.

"We open at eleven!" The woman turned away and proceeded to wipe down the railing.

"Let us in! We're from the Protectorate! Let us in!"

The woman threw down her rag. "The Protectorate! Linny! Come quickly!" She opened the inner door and passed through an enclosed foyer to the second, which opened outward. "Come in, come in!"

"What's this, then?" Linny said as she approached. "The Protectorate, you say?"

Miss Kristian could not contain her tears. "We've travelled all night," she said. "We are in Canada, aren't we?"

"Yes, this is Canada," Linny said.

"I knew we could do it! You won't send us back, will you?"

"Nonsense! Deandra, let's pour these two some coffee. The Protectorate! Well, freeze my cheese! How did you get here? You look half dead! Are you hungry?"

"Yes, ma'am," they replied together.

"Come with me," Linny said as she led them to a table where they could all sit, "and get out of those heavy clothes."

They took off their bulky snowsuits and placed them on the back of a nearby chair before settling in. Deandra served hot drinks and scones, and the two women joined them at the table.

Grateful to be off their feet after their long trek, Miss Kristian expressed their thanks and said a prayer before breaking off a corner of her scone. The coffee was bitter and neither was sure what to make of it, but they both sipped it slowly and told their harrowing tale of crossing Lake Superior.

"That's quite a story," Deandra said. "Linny, let's signal Bill. He can haul in their snowmobile."

Linny pushed up her sleeve and revealed a device that reminded Miss Kristian of Mrs. Stewart's watch.

"What's that?" Miss Kristian asked. She shot a questioning look at Miss Rhona.

"A SigProLite," Linny said, and saw their confusion, "so we can signal the guys. You know? Signal?"

Miss Kristian and Miss Rhona turned to one another, but said nothing.

"Look."

She leaned toward them revealing a small screen attached to her wrist strap. Linny swiped her finger across it, responding to flashing colored lights with the tip of her pointed fingernail.

"Hello?" A man's voice sounded from the device.

"Bill, can you come down to the restaurant? Tell you when you get here. And bring Trevin."

"On my way."

Miss Kristian was speechless, but Miss Rhona brightened up. "Can you signal anyone? We need to find someone…Miss Kristian's mother. She lives in…"

"Neebing! Signal Neebing!"

"What's her name?

"Zarah Browne." Miss Kristian spelled it out.

Linny taped on her screen. "That's a common name. I show four in the area, but no one in Neebing. Do you have her address?"

"No."

"We have a picture," Miss Rhona said. "You might recognize her."

"May I see?"

Miss Kristian pulled out her precious photograph. "It's twenty years old."

Linny glanced at the picture and held it near her device. "I'm scanning it in," she said, and then handed it back. More lights flashed as Linny tapped her screen. "Ah! A hit."

"Hello, this is Zarah." Linny turned her SigProLite toward Miss Kristian. "Hello? Who's there?"

"Say something."

Miss Kristian faltered. She swallowed and began again. "This is Miss Kristian."

"I'm sorry, who's that?"

"Your daughter? Miss Kristian."

There was silence. Miss Kristian's lower lip trembled and sweat formed along her neck.

"Kristian! My Kristian?"

Miss Kristian's throat tightened with emotion, "Mother!"

"My baby!" she sobbed.

Miss Kristian embraced Miss Rhona and wept while Linny finished the conversation. They made it, and that was all that mattered. Her mother would come soon to take them to her home, their new home; a place that would truly be superior.

Short story romance e-book titles
by Zoe Amos

Crossing the Bridge

Flow Like a River

Good Folk

Northern Belle

Oh, my Dog!

Second Chance

Stray Thoughts

White Shoulders

You

About the Author:

Zoe Amos writes short stories and novel-length fiction, as well as non-fiction articles and blog posts. Her short stories have been published in numerous anthologies by Alyson Books, Here Media, and Cleis Press.

Zoe Amos is the pen name of **Janet F. Williams**, author of the award-winning, non-fiction book, *"You Don't Ask, You Don't Get: Proven Techniques to Get More Out of Life."* Kirkus Indie named the book "Best Specialized Instruction Book" of 2010, a Top 10 Book of the Year. It was also named Finalist in the San Diego Book Awards and the Eric Hoffer Book Awards for Excellence in Independent Book Publishing in the self-help category.

Please connect with Zoe Amos on Facebook: Zoe.Amos. Author and on Twitter: @WhoisZoeAMOS. For more writing, please search for Zoe Amos by name. Read her blog posts on lesbian.com. E-mail: info@GoodDayMedia.com.

www.ingramcontent.com/pod-product-compliance
Lightning Source LLC
Chambersburg PA
CBHW060823120626
46557CB00001B/339